D.A. Dwinell

Bloom of Dreams

Guardian of the Stone
BOOK ONE

Chyanne,
    May God pour his blessings on you.
        Love,
        Dana Dwinell

D.A. Dwinell
Bloom of Dreams
This book is a work of fiction, and the events, incidents, locations, and characters are products of the author's imagination or are used fictitiously. Any resemblance to actual persons, living or dead, businesses, companies, organizations, events, or locales is entirely coincidental.
Copyright © 2020, DA Dwinell
Self-published

All rights reserved.
All rights reserved without limiting the rights under copyright reserved above, no part of the publication may be reproduced, stored in, or introduced into a retrieval system, or transmitted, in any form or by any means (electronic, mechanical, photocopy, recording or otherwise), without the prior written permission of the copyright owned and the publisher of the book.
First Printing, 2021

Special thanks to my dear friend Audrey Rich for her guidance and advice. I would also like to thank my father, Stephanie, and Tim for their honest critiques. To my family, I dedicate this book.

One

Sitting next to my mother, in front of my grandmother's casket, listening to Pastor Ellis, I realize it is just Mom and me now. It had been the three of us. Strands of hair brushed Mom's face from the light breeze. My mother stared at the casket. She appeared to be in another world. I watched as a tear fell down her cheek.

My grandmother would have loved the weather today. The sun was glowing. Fresh-cut grass filled the air. I sat there thinking about the faces I had seen when we arrived. Most were strangers. *Who are they to my grandmother?*

The news of her passing shocked us. My grandmother was so adventurous. Despite her age, she was always willing to try new things. She had an amazing ability to captivate her audience when she told stories. She made you want to believe they were real, but I always knew they were fictional. Her stories made you feel as though you were there with her. Mom and I always told her she should write books. Regrettably, she never did.

My mother was not like us. She was more reserved. A by-the-book type that did not like to be out of her comfort zone. My mother was only like us in appearance. She has always been the most conservative person I knew. She never wanted to leave the safety of the invisible box she had created for herself. She also worried a lot about everything. As I have gotten older, she has been a little less protective of me, because when she holds me back, I become withdrawn and depressed.

After my father passed, she was extremely protective and did not let me grieve the way I wanted. My depression during that time scared her. The therapist told her she needed to let me be me. Once she stopped smothering me and stopped trying to protect me from everything, I became better. Dealing with the loss of a parent is difficult, I needed to grieve in my own way.

When the service concluded, I stood next to my mother as she said her goodbyes, my dress blowing gently in the breeze, and thinking this felt like a dream. I was still in shock about my grandmother's passing; I did not pay too much attention to the people that attended her service. As I listened to friends and family tell us how much they loved her, I observed two men wearing black by the road and it seemed like they had binoculars and watching us. *Why would anyone need binoculars in a cemetery?* They saw me looking in their direction and quickly stepped into their vehicle and drove off.

We slowly made our way back to our car, but neither of us said a word the entire way to my grandmother's home for what my mother referred to as "A Day to Remember." As we approached her house, I could see the wall of stones that line the sidewalk in front of her home. Atop the stones was a black iron fence that surrounds her three-story red brick home. We parked on the street to allow our guests to park in the driveway.

We ambled up the path, my mother opened the iron gate headed up the stairs that led to the front door, but I slowed my pace and looked up to the double wooden doors where my grandmother normally would have been waiting for us with open arms. My feet stopped moving as I realized I will never again see her beautiful smile or hear more of her wonderful stories. My mind flashed with memories of the many fun times we had together.

She and I were so much alike. Both so curious about things we did not know about. Compassionate women, always fighting for the underdog, and we love adventure. Like Grandma, my zest for life drives me. People always told us we looked alike. The more I thought about her, the more emotional I became. My eyes teared up and when I blinked, a tear fell slowly down my face.

My mother spun around, "Are you okay?"

I looked up at her, "Yes." I wiped the tear from my cheek, knowing I was not okay. I needed to be strong for her because, like me, she was struggling with this loss.

My mom made a beeline toward the kitchen. I entered the foyer and spotted the flowers, which seem to be a few days old on the antique claw foot table. In front of me was the grand staircase. I spent many days as a young child playing on them and made my mother crazy running up and down them. To my left was the drawing-room, as Grandma called it. I remember hearing many of her stories as we snuggled on the sofa.

I walked toward the back of the house. Catching a glimpse of myself in the mirror above the desk, I noticed I was a bit of a mess. My long straight light brown hair was a little wind-blown from being at the cemetery. I began running my fingers through it to make it more presentable. I noticed my blue eyes, normally sparkled, are tired and dull. I wiped the smudged mascara from beneath my eyes and remembered how similar my eyes are to my grandmother's.

I turned toward the back of the house and passed the grand piano. I pictured my grandmother sitting on the piano bench. I could hear her playing, "Somewhere Over the Rainbow." Being that she loved that song, she would play it often. I remember her trying frequently to teach me to play. She even offered to pay for classes for me. My mother was immensely proud and always turned her down. My mom always said, "If I can't afford it, I don't need it." A beautiful flower arrangement sat in the center of the dining room table. My grandmother loved fresh flowers. When I reached the doorway to the kitchen, I noticed my mother looked older than her forty-six years. Her mother's death was taking a toll on her.

I could only imagine what it was like to lose a mother. My mother and I get along great, but we are so different. Our personalities were complete opposites. Her brown hair was just past her shoulders and had a bit of a wave to it. Our facial features were similar. People thought we looked alike despite our hair and eye color being different. My mother has the most amazing green eyes. People frequently complimented her on them. I was told she got those from her dad. My blue eyes came from my grandmother. My mother and grandmother both stood 5'6", I am a mere 5'4" and I must admit it has bothered me a lot. Mom still has a beautiful figure. Despite her beauty, she dated little since my father and her divorced.

As the doorbell chimed, Mom hollered for me to answer it. She was so engrossed in what she was doing; she did not notice me standing in the doorway. I headed to the door to make sure our guests did not need to wait long. I opened the door to find Pastor Ellis and his wife, Barbara, along with another couple standing there.

Pastor Ellis's blue eyes twinkled as he adjusted his baggy suit. "Brooke, it is nice to see you again."

Being surprised he remembered my name because I have not spoken with him in years, I said," It's nice to see you again." They seemed to know their way around. Barbara proceeded to the kitchen with a casserole dish and the Pastor, and the other couple headed to the drawing-room.

Just as I was about to close the front door, Brenda Smith placed her hand to stop it from shutting, "Well look at you, sweet pea."

I opened the door for Brenda, my mother's best friend from school. She was an amiable lady but always seemed a little on the wild side to be hanging out with mom. Mom's conservativeness helped keep Brenda out of trouble. She carried herself well in her black low-cut top and leopard print skirt with high heels. Her fashionable hairstyle flattered her face. It was shorter in the back and came down to her shoulders in the front.

"Thank you for coming, Ms. Brenda," I replied.

Brenda looked me over. "You are growing into a beautiful young lady. How old are you now, Brooke?"

"Seventeen," I said, but she did not seem interested because she was already making her way into the drawing-room.

I headed back to the kitchen to help my mother. She asked me to make sure everyone had a drink, which I did. The house filled with many of my grandmother's friends.

She had many friends in the area because she had lived in the area her entire life. It was nice to hear the stories about what a wonderful and caring person she was. I spent the rest of the evening filling drinks and cleaning up after our guests, wishing Phyllis were here. Not to do dishes, I just missed her.

Phyllis is my grandmother's best friend, but also her cook and housekeeper. Over the years, the two of them were inseparable. She became like another grandmother to me. Not only is she fun to be around and what little I knew how to cook, I learned from her. She lives here at my grandmother's home, but she is dealing with a family emergency and cannot be with us today. It must be important because she would be here if she could.

After everyone left, my mother told me our suitcases are in our rooms and to head to bed because we need to be at the attorney's office for the reading of the will first thing in the morning.

Climbing the stairs, I admired the decorative wood staircase that wrapped around the center of the home. It reaches to the third-floor. On the ceiling of the third-floor, a crystal chandelier that sparkles like diamonds. As a child, I pretended the prisms of light were stars dancing on the walls.

I would peek over the balcony to the first floor to see if my grandmother had changed the flowers from the day prior. My grandmother's home was the most beautiful home I had ever been in, and despite my modest upbringing, I have always felt at home here. Scanning the room, I remembered so many beautiful memories.

We usually came up for Christmas and spring break for our vacation. The main floor rooms are just off the hallway that leads from the foyer to the kitchen. Large wooden pocket doors greet you as you enter the dining room and drawing-room. They complement the wood door frames and hardwood floors. The only times I remember these doors being closed were my tenth birthday and every Christmas morning. I could not open the doors until everyone was there to see the doors opened, which revealed all the gifts under the tree. The rooms have beautiful accent rugs from my grandmother's travels.

As I approached the second floor, I passed the window seat, which has four stained glass windows behind it. Each window has the same stain glass pattern; red, pink, and white glass in the center, and the outer frame of each window was glass with both blue and green. The seat had pillows lined along with it. I had spent hours here listening to my grandmother while she told me stories of her adventures. She created a fictional world where villains chased her. She always defeated them. Occasionally, we would read books from her library.

My mother and I each have our rooms on the second floor. My grandmother and Phyllis have rooms on the third-floor. Mom tried persuading her to move to a room on the second floor. My grandmother would always say, "Walking up the three flights keeps me young."

My room was on the second floor to the right. Two gold high-back chairs and a small coffee table sat in the corner. A dresser sat on the wall between two windows. There are side tables on both sides of my queen-size bed. All antiques, just like the other furnishings in the home. Just off my room is a large closet, bathroom, and private balcony. The balcony has wooden plank flooring, and a stone and brick railing. The balcony furniture was beginning to show its age from the suns' hot rays and the rain hitting the pillows on the chairs. Many years ago, my mother let me have this room because I loved being outside enjoying the fresh air. She would often find me on the balcony reading a book or listening to music. My bathroom has a fireplace, which was rarely used.

My mother came over and hugged me. "I am so grateful for you, Brooke. I look at you and see my mother's spirit in you." she said with a smile on her face. "Now go to bed. Tomorrow's going to be another hard day." She gently closed the door.

Two

The next morning, I sprung out of bed as soon as my alarm went off and dressed. I made sure I was ready to head out before I made my way downstairs. As I walked down the hall, it sounded like my mother was still in her room. Mom had the weather report for the day on full blast. It's how she starts her day. I am greeted with the wonderful smell of bacon as I continued down the stairs. As I walked to the kitchen to see if my mother had made breakfast before getting ready, I noticed the drawing and dining room had been cleaned up by someone.

When I entered the kitchen, to my surprise, Phyllis was scrambling eggs. Despite having worked as a housekeeper and cook for my grandmother for as long as I can remember, she's family. Phyllis, a thin woman with dark hair. She frequently wore it up in a high bun. She also inherited her mother's Asian traits. Her mother was from Japan and her father was a white veteran from Kentucky and they met when he was stationed in Japan. You would never have guessed from looking at her she is in her sixties. Not only did she look much younger than her age, but she also had a lot of energy.

I ran over and hugged her as if I never wanted to let her go.

Phyllis pulled back and looked me over with an enormous smile. "I have missed you, sweet child," she said as she pulled me back to her and hugged me. "I am sorry I was not at the funeral yesterday. You know I would not intentionally miss your grandma's funeral, but my sister fell ill yesterday morning, and I had to take her to the hospital." She continued, as she turned to make me a plate of scrambled eggs, biscuits with gravy, and bacon.

"Thank you for breakfast." I grabbed my plate. "Mom told me about your sister. I hope she feels better soon. Has Mom eaten yet?" I asked as I took a bite from my bacon.

"She came down for coffee and said she wasn't hungry and went back to her room. Now hurry up your mother will be down soon," Phyllis said as she cleaned the kitchen.

My grandmother and Phyllis were so close. Phyllis knows more about her than anyone else. They spent a lot of time together. Phyllis would even chime in during my grandmother's stories and add special details. Grandma rarely took trips without her. They traveled the world together. I am sure Phyllis has wonderful stories to tell. My grandmother tried telling her she did not need to work for her because she was more than a housekeeper, but Phyllis insisted and told her she enjoyed working for her but would always be her friend.

As I finished my meal, I heard heels clicking on the hardwood floors. I quickly rinsed off my plate and put it in the dishwasher.

"Good morning, Brooke. How are you feeling today?" my mother asked, as she picked a piece of lint from her skirt.

"I am doing okay. I was enjoying reminiscing with Phyllis," I said as I kissed Phyllis on the cheek.

My mother thanked Phyllis for everything and told her we would help clean the kitchen when we returned from the attorney's office.

Phyllis, my mother, and I arrived at the Law Offices of Smith, Stine, and Thomas. We entered the large entryway and were greeted by the receptionist.

"I am Sandra Davis to see Mr. Thomas," my mother advised her.

The receptionist nodded and picked up the phone, and said, "Your appointment is here."

As Mr. Thomas entered the room, I remembered him being at the funeral. He was a tall, handsome man with a nice build. His blue suit fit him too well and must have been custom-made. He greets us, before leading us to a large conference room. The table could accommodate enough seating for twenty. It made me feel insignificant compared to it. One wall was covered in law books, the other had a counter with coffee and ice water for clients, which Mr. Thomas offered us. We sat for the reading of the will. Mr. Thomas brushed his hand through his brown hair as he explained we were the only people mentioned in the will.

Had my grandmother willed something to me? If so, what? I was sure my mother would get everything.

As Mr. Thomas discussed with us the first few pages of the will, cover the normal things, outstanding bills, funeral costs, etc. He excused himself from the room, swiftly returning with a locked case. He addressed Phyllis, "Ms. Lillie Davis willed you a sum of $65,000 and this envelope, which you may only share with Brooke if you choose to. You must read it while you are here, and we will burn it when you are finished."

Phyllis took the letter and walked to the other side of the room. She did nothing other than nod her head. She put the letter back in the envelope and walked back to join us.

Phyllis just stood at the table for a minute. She turned to me, "I think you should read this Brooke." She handed me the letter. Following her lead, I walked away from the table. *What could this letter possibly say?* I opened the envelope and began reading.

> My dearest Phyllis,
> You are my dearest friend, and you hold so many of my secrets. It was a blessing having you on my many adventures. I will always love you and cherish our friendship. Brooke is to inherit my most prized item and will soon learn of its power and her destiny. I ask you to help guide and be there for her as you were for me.
> Love,
> Lillie

Power? My destiny? What is she talking about? I read the letter again, which did not help me understand it any better. I gazed up at Phyllis, who looked back with a smile.

Mr. Thomas placed a trash can on the counter and asked me for the letter. I handed it to him. He lit the letter, dropped it in the can, and fanned the smoke to keep the detectors from going off. He sat and read from the will again, "Brooke, your grandmother has set up a trust for you. It will pay for all your college expenses and should leave you with approximately $250,000 after college expenses. These funds will not be distributed until you obtain the age of twenty-five. In addition to the funds, your grandmother has willed you her most cherished necklace and an antique compact mirror." He reached into the case and pulled out a dark leather box that looked incredibly old. He handed the box to me, along with a sterling silver mirror, and an envelope. My grandmother had used this mirror for years. I have even used it from time to time. As I held the mirror, I softly rubbed my fingers across the top of the mirror as I thought about how she always had it with her.

"The rules for your letter are the same. As soon as you finish reading the letter, the letter must be destroyed," he stated as he motioned toward the previously burned letter.

Adding to my confusion, I put the mirror next to the box on the table and opened the envelope.

My dearest Brooke,
   You have been the light of my life. I am going to share my most cherished gift with you. You may ask why you and not your mother? I tried for many years to have Sandra open her mind to things to prepare her for what I am about to tell you, but she is so closed-minded. This gift would be wasted on her. You must be incredibly careful who you share this secret with. Many may try to take this gift from you or even try to kill you, but you must protect it with your life. The necklace you just received is my most cherished possession, it is not just any necklace; it is known as the Bloom of Dreams. We have passed this stone through our family for generations. My mother passed it on to me. The person who wears this necklace can travel the world and it will also let you know when trouble is approaching. The stories I told you are not fiction. They are all true. Phyllis can help guide you until you find out how to use the stone. One day you will need to pass this on to one of your ancestors. Choose this person wisely.
   You are now the protector of the Bloom of Dreams. I task you with not only protecting the stone, but you must use it for good. Please speak with Phyllis before wearing the necklace and stay safe.
With all my love,
Grandma

Her stories are true? How can this be? Bloom of Dreams, what is that? What did she mean, many may come to take it? Why do I need to protect it with my life? Stay safe? From what...the people trying to kill me? My heart was racing. I began to feel sick to my stomach. I have so many questions. I need to get Phyllis alone to get answers. *Why does Phyllis know so much?*

Mr. Thomas asked if I finished reading the letter. I nodded and before I knew it; he took the letter, and it was destroyed.

My mother turned to me and asked me to open the box. You could tell she seemed confused as well. I slowly opened it. Nestled inside light blue satin was a dark blue round stone that resembled a flower. The stone resembles the star sapphire. The necklace was made of sterling silver. The pendant has a unique pattern of silver wire. It did not have a constant pattern circling it. The silver linked around and twisted at various points which connected the metal. I recognized this necklace because my grandmother always wore it. As I looked over it, my mother said, "My mother has had this my entire life. I rarely have seen her without it."

I wanted to put it on, but I refrained and turned to my mother, "I can't believe she gave this to me."

Mr. Thomas asked, "Are we ready to continue?"

My mother and I nodded and turned our attention to Mr. Thomas. He continued reading from the will. This time addressing my mother's inheritance, "Sandra, your mother has gifted you her home and all assets that are not in trust or that were already mentioned."

My mother and Mr. Thomas needed to finish discussing what those assets were, so Mr. Thomas excused Phyllis and me from the conference room. We made our way to the door. I could not wait to get her alone to discuss the information in my letter. As we exited the building, the sun began warming my skin and cooled by the light breeze in the air. I took a minute to take it in while trying to compose my thoughts. Phyllis sat on a bench in front of the building. The tree provided much-needed shade over the bench. As I looked over at Phyllis, I could tell she deeply missed my grandma. We are all trying to be strong for one another. I sat beside her and placed my hand on hers. "Ms. Phyllis, are you okay?" I asked.

She placed her other hand on mine and said, "I will be fine. I miss your grandmother, but I have lost many loved ones in my lifetime. I've been blessed to know such an amazing woman." Phyllis looked me in the eye and pushed the strands of hair away from my eye before continuing, "Lillie always told me she fell in love with you the day she held you the first time. She has known for many years that you were to replace her. She was planning on telling you everything on your eighteenth birthday." Phyllis took a deep breath and said," Now, I suggest you ask me what is on your mind because we don't have much time before your mother and Mr. Thomas finish the paperwork."

Surprised at her bluntness, I asked, "The letter I received was about the necklace and my grandmother's secret. Grandma said the stories she told me were true. How can this be and why are people going to come after the stone?"

Phyllis takes another deep breath as though she was searching for words and replies, "Yes, the stories are true, I know because I accompanied her on several journeys when we were much younger. The Bloom of Dreams holds special powers that allow you to transport yourself, and to explore this world in unique ways."

How could this be true, I wondered?

She continued, "Whoever wears the pendant must have a good heart and must never use it for evil. Tonight, after your mother goes to bed, I will come to you in your room to show you how it works, promise me you will not wear the necklace until then."

"I promise. Grandma mentioned I must protect it with my life. Who is going to come after it?" I inquired with concern.

"The Bloom of Dreams is not known by many, but there are those who know what power it possesses, and they have been trying to take it from this family since they discovered it. When you wear the stone, you will have special powers. You must always have your guard up and never leave the Bloom of Dreams just anywhere. I encourage you to learn skills to protect yourself."

The front door of the law firm opened, and my mother emerged. She motioned for us to head to the car. On the ride home I found myself staring at the necklace and the mirror thinking about the many stories my grandmother shared with me. She often spoke of the Granaldi's attacking her.

Was that a warning for me to be aware of them?

Three

We arrived back at my grandmother's home. My mother told me she and Phyllis would take care of the dishes and I needed to head upstairs to study for my final exams. As I headed to my room, a text came in from my best friend Mechelle Garcia. We have known each other since middle school. She had long hair with loose curls and brown eyes. We were the same physical size, and we often shared clothes.

MECHELLE: I haven't heard from you. R U OK?

I grabbed my history book and my phone and called from my balcony.

Mechelle picked up the phone, "I'm worried about you. What's up?"

I told her about the funeral and our trip to the attorney's office. Briefly mentioning the necklace, mirror, and that my grandmother would pay for college. Making sure the part about it having special powers was excluded from our conversation.

She said, "That's great! That'll help you and your mother out. Have you decided what school you're going to?"

"I don't want to abandon my mom because she needs me. If she moves to Louisville and lives in my grandmother's house, I will stay in Louisville with her and attend the University of Louisville. If we stay in Florida, I will go to Florida Atlantic University. I will just live with her there." I replied.

"What do ya think she'll do?" Mechelle inquired.

"Don't know. There's no way I will pressure her for an answer. I'll be back in time for our final exams. Speaking of exams, I need to study," I said, before ending the call. I picked up my history book and began studying.

Phyllis made us fried chicken, mashed potatoes, and fried okra for dinner. It was delicious. It appears she is making sure we have comfort foods while we are here. As we ate dinner, my mother asked me how I would feel about making this our permanent home. Deep down, I was hoping she would want to move here. I have always loved Kentucky. It would be hard to part with this house. I replied,

"I'd be fine with that. I've so many fond memories of being here, and I was already considering going to the University of Louisville."

She asked, "Are you sure? You would be leaving all of your friends in Florida."

"Most are going away to college and won't be there most of the time. Besides, here we've got Ms. Phyllis, what would she do if we didn't come here. I don't want to lose her."

Phyllis, who was joining us for dinner, smiled at me. Her eyes watering up told me she liked my response. After dinner, I headed to my room to study some more. I returned to the balcony with my books. As I walked outside, I noticed a boy next door working on his truck. He was hanging over the side of his truck wearing old jeans and cowboy boots. His white t-shirt and ball cap looked like they had seen better days. Although I could only see his profile, he was attractive. I think he could feel me staring at him because he glanced up in my direction and when we made eye contact; he nodded his head as to say hello. Knowing he caught me spying on him, I waved at him awkwardly before retreating to my chair. I attempted to study but wanted to get another glimpse of the attractive stranger. I quietly leaned over the balcony to see if I could catch another look. A teenage girl with long brown hair walked up to him. She knocked off his ball cap, which revealed his brown hair, short on the sides and was a little longer on top. They chatted. I could not hear what they were saying, but they were laughing. I am guessing this mystery man has a girlfriend. Feeling disappointed, I returned to my studies before I'm caught again.

Before heading to bed, I made my way to the kitchen for a snack. My mother was at the dining room table going through my grandmother's mail. She seemed a bit overwhelmed. "I am getting a snack; would you like something to eat?"

"Phyllis baked a peach pie before heading to bed," she replied. I hurried to the kitchen and cut us both a slice. I returned to the dining room and put my mother's slice in front of her before sitting across from her.

Mom raises her head from her papers and says, "I think Phyllis cooks to take her mind off things. I feel bad that I am not up to eating, but I know it would please her if we enjoyed a slice." Mom took a few bites of the pie and pushed it aside. "We're heading home the day after tomorrow so you won't miss your final exams, and we will stay until your graduation. Giving us time to pack the things we need and donate the things we don't. I also need to find a job. Do you want to bring your bedroom furniture here or would you rather use the furniture that's already in your room?"

I realized I love the room here. The furniture at home is in poor condition, but it's better than what someone less fortunate might have. "I'm happy with the room here. I'd like to bring some of my personal items," I said as I created a list in my head of what needed to be packed.

"You're right. We shouldn't bring any furniture with us because the things here are much nicer than anything we have, which will make it easier for us to get back up here. With us heading back here after graduation, we'll be celebrating your eighteenth birthday in Kentucky. Are you okay with that?" she asked.

"Yes, that means Phyllis can make me one of her special cakes," I said knowing that in my heart I would have liked to spend it with my friends in Florida, but I want to make this as easy of a transition for my mother as possible.

After washing our dishes, I headed to my room, not knowing when Phyllis would arrive or if she had just gone to bed. I stared at the necklace, wondering what would happen if I put it on, but also fearful that something dreadful would happen if I did. It was about 11:30 pm when there was a gentle knock on my door. It was my mother, saying goodnight before heading to her room. Phyllis's room was on the third-floor, just down the hall from my grandmother's room. I thought about running up to her room, but I did as I was told and waited for her to come to me. I tried to study, to take my mind off everything that was revealed to me in the letter from my grandmother, but no matter how hard I tried, I could not focus. The sound of a creek in the floorboards alerted me of Phyllis's presence outside my door. I glanced at the clock. It was 12:36 am when Phyllis slowly opened my door.

Four

She entered and said, "I wanted to make sure your mother was asleep before coming down." Phyllis made herself comfortable in one of the gold high-back chairs on the other side of the room.

I grabbed the box, which still held the necklace, and sat in the chair next to her. She noticed the mirror was sitting on the dresser in the room and motioned toward it. "You need to get the mirror also," she said.

The mirror? What does the mirror have to do with the necklace? Were they connected somehow? I swiftly grabbed the mirror and returned to my seat. Phyllis took the box from me and carefully took the necklace from its bed in the light blue satin. "The Bloom of Dreams is more valuable than anything you'll ever own. You must not abuse the powers it provides you and you must protect it with your life."

What has my grandmother given me and how did she come to get this?

Phyllis motioned for me to lean toward her. She placed the necklace around my neck. Expecting something magical to happen, I felt nothing other than the coldness of the stone on my chest. I inspected the stone to see if there was a difference with it, but nothing had happened with it either. *Should something be happening?*

She took the mirror I had placed on the table in front of us, "This is especially important. Whenever you leave this house, you must always carry the mirror with you. Make sure you protect it as well. This mirror will always help bring you to a safe place."

What? How is a mirror going to bring me anywhere? I'm so confused. I refrain from asking and let Phyllis continue.

She grabbed my hand and led me to the full-length mirror in my room. "I want you to think about the home your parents had before the divorce. There was a tall tree in the backyard next to the fence. Now, picture the area just next to the tall tree."

In my mind I pictured it, and as it became more in focus, I could feel Ms. Phyllis clinging to my arm. I pictured the light grey stucco on the house and the screened-in patio. I saw the image in the mirror change and it revealed my house. *How is my house inside the mirror?* My eyes shot over to Phyllis. She told me to step into the mirror.

Is she crazy? I cannot step into the mirror. Frozen in place, wondering what to do, when I saw her step through the mirror and pull me through.

My foot felt the cool damp grass beneath it. I was in the backyard of my first home. A chill ran through me. I peeked over at Phyllis and asked her if this was real. She walked me over to the side of the house where we had kept our garbage cans. I remembered Mom always fussing about the cans sitting in the dirt, so dad made a small patio for them. Phyllis quietly moved a garbage can to reveal two small handprints and the year my father had written on the cement when he made it. I reached down to touch the prints that I had placed there. *How could this be happening?* Phyllis told me we needed to return home. She handed me the mirror and grabbed my arm. I commented, "I stepped into the mirror to get here. I can't step into this mirror it is too small."

In a quiet voice, Phyllis said, "Look into it as you did when you arrived here and think about where you want to be, and it will take you there. If you choose to be invisible when you arrive at your destination, it will make you invisible, but you must picture yourself arriving that way. Do not misuse the stone. This small mirror will pull you into it. You can use any reflection to teleport yourself. Lillie has used the water fountain in the backyard on several occasions. However, you can only transport to places you have seen. If you need to go somewhere, you have never been, you will need to locate a picture of the place to use as your image to focus on."

I stared at the mirror and picturing my room and with no notice I could feel myself being sucked into it and spit out. Phyllis and I both landed on the floor. I arose and helped her up.

Phyllis sat down in the yellow chair and said, "We must talk about the Bloom of Dreams. Your grandmother was a protector of the Bloom, and now you have taken over as the protector. In 1889, your great-great-great-grandfather, purchased the ring which contained the stone. After he discovered the power of the ring, he vowed never to tell anyone of its existence and to only use it for good, but in order to save a man's life he revealed its powers to this man. We do not know why, but he removed the stone from the ring and created the necklace you are now wearing. Lillie believed the Granaldis have the original ring. It is also said that the stone lost some of its powers when it was removed from the ring. She told me the setting that holds the Bloom of Dreams is known as the Bloom's Cradle. Each protector must choose a successor from their family to take over as protector before they pass. Your grandmother planned to tell you about the necklace prior to her death. For your graduation present she was going to take you to Italy and tell you about it and her desire to have you as its protector. Unfortunately, she passed before that could happen. With your grandmother's recent passing, you must be incredibly careful of strangers trying to get the stone. The few that know of its existence will try to find it or to find out who now has possession of it. The mirror will bring you to the location of your choosing. If anyone is touching you while you use the stone, they will go with you to the new destination. Therefore, I urge you not to use it if someone evil may be near you. You must protect the Bloom of Dreams with your life as well as the cradle if you locate it."

I glanced at the clock. "Phyllis it is 1:18 in the morning."

She says, "Yes, now go to bed and get some rest. We both need to get up early in the morning." Phyllis left my room, and I noticed dirt on my feet and pajamas. Quickly cleaned my feet and changed into a new set of pajamas before I slipped into bed. As I laid there thinking about what had just occurred, I had so many questions for my grandmother. A tear fell down my cheek because I could not ask her any of them. With all that had occurred in the past few days, exhausted, I quickly fell asleep.

Five

I woke up to the sound of my bedroom door opening.

"Good morning, sweetheart. You are sleeping in late today. Are you feeling, okay?" my mother inquired.

Trying to wake me up, I remembered what had happened the night before. *Was it a dream?*

My mother sat next to me on the bed and brushed the hair from my eyes. "It is nice to see you wearing your grandmother's necklace. The blue in it brings out the blue in your eyes," She pulls the sheets off me and told me to head down as soon as I am dressed.

I showered and noticed my pajamas in the hamper as I dried my hair. The dirt from the yard was on them, just as it was when we returned last night. *Last night was real!* I dressed and headed downstairs to find Phyllis.

Mom was at the dining room table making a list and drinking coffee when she said, "Phyllis went to see her sister and will be out all day. I have a few chores to take care of before heading home tomorrow. Your grandmother wanted her clothing donated to Women Against Abuse. Would you mind packing them up for me?", she asked just before her phone rang and took the call.

I grab an apple and yogurt for breakfast before returning to the dining room when I heard my mother say, "Are you okay, Mr. Thomas?"

I return to the dining room where my mother looked concerned. She was listening intently. Before hanging up the phone she said, "We will, thank you again."

I asked if everything was okay.

She told me what happened, "Mr. Thomas told me that a couple of people came to his office today asking questions about your grandmother. They inquired about her will. They demanded a copy. They beat him before he gave them the will. He said he notified the police about the incident, but he wanted to make sure we were aware of what happened."

"Why would anyone care about Grandma's will?" I asked, knowing that this might have something to do with the Bloom of Dreams.

She looked puzzled and said, "I haven't a clue. Hurry and get the clothes packed. Phyllis said there are boxes in the garage. I am going to run my errands quickly. Call me if the police show up and if you see anything suspicious call the police." She ripped off the top sheet of paper with her to-do list and headed toward her car.

I hurried to the garage to find some boxes and discovered my grandmother's silver Cadillac. I found the boxes. I was about to close the garage door when I felt someone behind me. My first thought was of the people that attacked Mr. Thomas. I quickly dropped the boxes and turned, ready to punch anyone in my way.

The handsome boy from next door retreating from my swing. I could now see how truly handsome he is. He had a nice tan and green eyes that were a different shade of green than my mother's. I could tell he is fit by his build.

"Do you always attack your neighbors?" he asked with the cutest smile that showed his amazing dimples.

Embarrassed by what had just occurred, I snapped, "Do you always sneak up on people and scare them to death?"

"Let's start over, I live next door. My name is Greg. I heard that Ms. Lillie passed. I am guessing you are related to her," he said with a smile that made my knees feel weak.

I leaned over and picked up one of my boxes and replied, "Lillie was my grandmother."

Greg leaned over and picked up the other two boxes that still lay on the ground, "I did not know her very well. We just moved into the neighborhood a few months ago. I attend the University of Louisville and my parents wanted me to be closer to the college. We moved here from Mount Washington."

I motioned to have him hand me the box.

He pulled the box away from my reach, "No, I got this. Lead the way."

He seemed charming and appears to be a gentleman. I led him into the house and up to my grandmother's room on the third-floor.

I noticed Greg taking in the home's grandeur. "Whoever did the woodwork in this house was a genuine artist," he stopped for a moment as he looked up the center of the stairs that led to the third-floor.

As we entered her room, I realized I had only been in this room with my grandmother. It is about the size of mine but has a four-poster wooden bed. Her dresser is near the window and there is a sitting area that has two chairs and a small sofa. The walls have deep red wallpaper; the bed is covered in pillows that complement the wall coloring, and the light beige colored comforter on the bed. There is a fireplace between the two windows the sofa faces. We put the boxes on the floor by the closet.

"Are you packing her things up?" he asked.

"Yes, she wanted them donated. I think my mother might move into her room when we come back," commenting as I opened a box.

"Are you moving here?" he asked.

I handed him clothes from the closet to put in the box and told him our plans. "We are heading back to Florida tomorrow. I have exams next week and after I graduate, we are moving here," I said, hoping that would make him happy. The smile that appeared on his face tells me it did, but I am sure his girlfriend would not approve of it.

We finished packing the closet and realized we need more boxes for the dresser. He thought he had some at his house and I know there were more in the garage. We moved a few packed boxes and left them in the foyer. We headed toward Greg's house. A car parked out front, with two men in it, who seemed to be watching my grandmother's house. As we walked by the vehicle, I noticed a bright red cooler in the back seat. *Who are these people?* I thought I am overthinking the situation. I moved my attention back to Greg who had been telling me about the type of boxes he thought he had in his garage. There were several boxes, and we put them just inside my back door before heading to my garage for the other boxes. Greg closed the garage, I looked up and found the two men still in the vehicle. They seem to watch our every move. Greg followed me back into the house. I locked the door behind him, to prevent anyone's entry.

He turned to me, "I don't know what people are like in Florida, but around here people leave their doors unlocked all the time."

I just smiled and confirmed I locked the door before following him back up to my grandmother's room. From the window in her room, I saw the vehicle. *Why are they here? What do they want?*

As we packed up the dresser, I noticed Greg watching the vehicle too. He continued packing until something caught his eye outside. He moved the curtain back from the window to get a better view. "Did you notice the vehicle out front?" he asked.

Making my way to the window to see what he was looking at; the two men jump out of the car and strode to my house. My palms sweat, as my mind started racing about the men. Even though Greg was here, my stomach started flip-flopping as I rubbed my clammy hands on my jeans. The doorbell chime rang. Frozen in place. *Are these the people Mom warned me about?*

Greg asked, "Are you going to get the door?"

I asked him to come downstairs, wondering if he could hear the nervousness in my voice. We made our way to the second floor. I grabbed my hoody from my bed and put it on before continuing downstairs to the first floor. Zipping the hoody to hide the Bloom of Dreams, I heard the chimes again and could see one man trying to look in the glass on the front door.

I grabbed Greg's hand, "Please stay right here." My body was so tense, I almost did not notice Greg seemed pleased that I held his hand.

I unlocked the door and opened it enough for them to see Greg was standing next to me. One has dark wavy hair, and they had similar features and appeared as if they might be of Italian descent. "Can I help you?" I asked and noted the stone under my hoody was heating. *Is this what Phyllis meant when she said the stone would warn me of danger?*

The gentleman on the right said, "Lillie was a friend of ours and we wanted to see how the family is doing. Are you Lillie's granddaughter Brooke?" He moved his gaze to my neck. Feeling self-conscious of him noticing my necklace, I adjusted my hoody to make sure the necklace stayed hidden.

"Where do you know Lillie from?" I asked, making sure I did not reveal my connection with her.

"Oh, we go way back," he said, trying to see inside the home, and he asked, "Can we come in?"

I said, "I am sorry, but I cannot let strangers in. I can give Sandra your name and number if you would like her to contact you."

The man on the left had a scar on his chin and dark eyes. He seemed displeased by my response, "We will come back later when she is home." He turned to the other man and motioned him to walk away.

I shut the door and locked it. The stone returns to its normal temperature as we climbed the stairs.

Greg said, "Did you find it odd that they would not give you their name and phone number?"

"Yes, very odd. Something tells me they knew my grandmother, but they were not friends," We finish packing the items in my grandmother's dresser. Greg helped me get the remaining boxes down the stairs. My legs burned from going up and down the stairs so much. We brought down the last box.

My mom came in from the back door and hollered, "Brooke!"

"We are in the foyer," I announced.

Gregory wiped the sweat off his hands on his jeans before my mother entered the hallway. She seemed surprised to see a stranger in the house. She asked, "Who do we have here?"

"This is Greg. He lives next door. He has been helping me with Grandma's things. We have everything packed," I motioned to the many boxes on the floor.

"Wow, you got a lot done while I was gone. Thank you for your help," Mom said as she shook his hand." Why don't you stay and join us for dinner? I was going to order pizza."

He looked over at me to see my response to her question. I smile, glad my mother had asked. "Yes, stay."

He grinned. "That sounds great. Do you mind if Brooke and I drop these boxes off for you?"

A smile came across my mother's face. "Yes, thank you. This gives me one less thing to worry about." She shot a look at me as if she is thinking, wow is he for real.

"I'll pull my truck up front so we can load it. I will be back in a minute," Greg said before heading out the front door.

Mom faces me and says, "Please explain the mystery man."

Mom seems impressed with Greg and probably wants to know if I am interested in him, but regrettably, I tell her, "Don't get your hopes up, I think he has a girlfriend."

Mom's face shows her disappointment. "That's too bad, I have a feeling he is a good kid." She begins telling me about the errands she has completed.

Six

A knock at the front door interrupted her. Mom opened the door to let Greg in, and to both of our surprise he was standing there with the girl I saw him with the other day. *How is it possible that she looks even more beautiful?*

Greg introduced us, "This is Karen, she is going to help us move these boxes."

My mother smiled, "Hello, Karen. It is nice of you both to come to help us."

His next words told me what I longed to hear.

"Mom raised us right. You always lend a helping hand to your neighbors in need," Greg said.

Did I hear that correctly? This is his sister. I smiled at her, "Yes, thank you for your help."

Mom helps us get the boxes into the bed of Greg's truck and gave us the address to deliver them. Karen insisted I sit up front with Greg. It was a short drive to the Women of Abuse Drop-Off Center, but that did not stop Karen from firing questions at me during the ride.

"Greg said, you are moving in next door after you graduate. What college are you planning on attending?" she asked.

When did he have time to fill her in? "I hadn't decided on a college until we decided to move here. I've been accepted to the University of Louisville and will start in the fall," I say proudly, knowing Greg is currently attending there.

Upon hearing this she shot a look at her brother, who was looking at her in the rear-view mirror, which told me she thought he is pleased with my answer. He took a sudden right, and the GPS started telling him to turn around. "Where are you going?" Karen asked.

"I think we are being followed," Greg replied as he was checking each of his mirrors.

"Is it the guys that showed up at the house today?" I asked with concern in my voice.

I could see the concern in Greg's face. Karen shouted as she looked around the vehicle, "What are you talking about? Who is following us?"

I explained to Karen about the two men that showed up early at my grandmother's house and our concern about the reasons for their visit. We turned left, and he pulled over. Greg and I looked for the vehicle to see if they would pass us, but I did not see the car make the turn. With a sigh of relief, Greg stated, "I think we lost them." He pulled back on the road and proceeds to the drop-off center.

Karen restarted her interrogation. "Is there a special guy back home?" she asked.

I peek at Greg to see what his face would tell me. "No." He seemed happy about my answer.

We arrived at the drop-off center and unloaded the boxes. I turned to Greg and said, "Is it me or do you feel like we are being watched?"

"I feel it too," he said as he appeared to be scanning the area. Once he finished, he faced me. "Perhaps we are letting our imagination get the best of us."

We piled into Greg's truck and headed back home. I asked Karen if she wanted to join us for dinner, but she said she promised to help her mother cook dinner and had homework to do. We arrived at home and Greg said he was going to clean himself up and would be over shortly. I headed into the house to tell my mother about the strangers that had come over. My mother was in the drawing-room with two gentlemen. I drew closer and realized these were the men that had come by earlier in the day. My first impulse was to run out the door and tell Greg they stopped following us because they are here now, but I knew I could not do that. My mother called out to me, "Brooke, please come into the drawing-room. We have guests."

I tried to collect myself because I did not want to scare my mother. My heart was racing to the point I might pass out and my hands trembled. Panic. It is so hard to breathe. *Calm down, Brooke.* I took a deep breath. I entered the room, and the stone warmed against my skin.

The necklace was so hot it felt as if it might burn me. *How do I get these men out of the house?* I must find a way, and quickly.

"Brooke, this is Tony and Joseph Granaldi."

I interrupted my mother. "Greg will be over any minute. He went home to clean up a bit before dinner. "Did you order the pizzas yet?"

Mom realized she had forgotten about dinner. She turned to our guests and asked if they would like to join us. Thankfully, they declined and thanked her for her time before heading to the front door. Trying to get them to leave, I opened the door to encourage them to stop talking and exit. Just as I opened the door, Greg walked up the path. The two men exited and nearly ran into Greg. Greg enters the house with a confused look and quietly asked me, "Why are they here?"

"Do you know them, Greg?" my mother asked as she shut the door.

He looked at me, seeming as though he did not know how to respond.

"They were here earlier today. After sitting in their car for nearly an hour, they came to the door. They wanted to know if I was Lillie's granddaughter and wanted me to let them into the house. We asked them to give us their name and number to provide to you, but they refused to, and I would not let them in," I replied for him.

Greg added, "We even had them following us when we left here. I lost them. They must've come here and try to get information out of you while we were gone."

"Mom, were they the men that attacked Mr. Thomas? Did he describe them to you?" I inquired.

"I don't think so. Please order the pizza and I will call Mr. Thomas," she instructed.

I placed the pizza order and returned to my mothers' side, anxiously wanting to hear what Mr. Thomas had to say. Just before hanging up the phone, she said," I'll call the police. Thank you, Mr. Thomas."

"They're the same men, aren't they?" I asked, feeling more nervous than ever.

"We don't know for sure," Mom said as she called the police.

I grabbed Greg's hand and led him to the kitchen to get us plates and drinks for dinner.

"Do you have any idea what these men want?" he asked.

After hearing their last name, I know they want the Bloom of Dreams, but I cannot disclose that to Greg or my mother. "I'm not sure, but I think it may have something to do with my grandmother," I informed him.

I poured sweet tea in each glass and Greg took them to the dining room while I got us plates and napkins. Mom entered the kitchen and explained the police would arrive shortly to take our statements. I grabbed the plates and headed to the dining room. The doorbell rang, and Mom answers the door. Mom and Greg returned to the dining room. Greg was holding the pizza and placed it on the table. We sat down and bowed our heads.

Mom proceeded to say grace, "Dear heavenly Father, thank you for all you are doing in our lives and for this food and the hands that prepared it. We ask that you lead us and guide us and protect us. Amen."

Everyone seemed hungry because they eagerly dug into the pizza. I turned to Mom and asked, "What time are we leaving in the morning?"

"With all that has been going on, I forgot we need to head home tomorrow. I would like to get an early start. How about 6:00 am?" she asked, but it was more like a statement.

We talked about the number of clothes my grandmother owned, and Greg told us a little about the University of Louisville before the doorbell rang. We all headed to the foyer to see if the police had arrived. Mom opened the door to discover a fit police officer with a touch of grey in his light brown hair. He introduced himself as Detective Roberts. Mom invited him in. She led him to the drawing-room. We all sat and provided the officer with the events of the day, including a detailed description of the two men and the names they provided to us.

The officer told us he will let us know if he finds anything out about them and lets himself out. Greg and I cleared the table and did the dishes, while Mom told us she was packing, and going to bed. Phyllis's car pulled into the driveway, so I unlocked the back door. She gave me a brief peck on the cheek, and said, "It's nice to see you, Gregory."

He smiled and said, "It's nice to see you, Ms. Phyllis."

Phyllis scanned the kitchen and said, "I will finish these up. You need to finish packing and get to bed early. You have a long day tomorrow."

I thanked her and walked Greg to the door. "Thank you for everything today," I said, not wanting him to leave but knowing Phyllis was correct, I needed to head to bed.

He said, "What are neighbors for. Besides, you lead an interesting life, Ms. Brooke. Never a dull moment." Greg and I exchanged numbers before he left.

Seven

The past few weeks have been a little hectic with final exams and trying to pack our home. Mom gave away things we will no longer want to our church members that are in need. Mechelle and I tried to spend time together, but she had been busy with her out-of-town family, and I have been helping Mom prepare for our move. Greg and I have been texting nearly every day. He's keeping an eye out for the Granaldi brothers and checking in daily on Phyllis. He told me her sister is doing much better.

    I have not used the Bloom of Dreams since the night Phyllis and I went to visit my childhood home, but I have not taken it off either. It is important to me Phyllis be with me when I try to use it again. My feelings are mixed. I am looking forward to seeing Greg and Phyllis, as well as starting a new chapter of my life. I was also looking forward to learning more about the Bloom of Dreams. However, I will miss my life in Florida, but most of my friends are heading out of town on their own adventures.

    The night before graduation, my mother told me she was taking me out for a farewell dinner and to put on a nice dress.

    I wore my blue sundress because it complemented the Bloom of Dreams. I glanced at myself in the mirror and realized I needed lip gloss. I searched through my purse to put on my favorite gloss, my grandmother's compact mirror was still there from my grandmother's house. It occurred to me I had forgotten about it with all that has been going on. It reminded me to have it with me all the time. I used it to apply the lip gloss. I was putting it back in my purse when someone knocked at the door. My mother hollered for me to answer it. I opened the door; surprised to see Mechelle. She wore a white off-the-shoulder scalloped trim top with a matching skirt and tan heels. The white brought out her beautiful tan skin.

    "You look great! Are you ready to go?" she asked.

    My mother walked in, "Surprise!" She gave me a side hug. "You girls have fun." She handed me money and returned to packing.

    We headed out to her car, I grabbed the door handle, "So, where are we headed?"

    Mechelle smiled and responded, "Bimini Twist."

    She knew me so well. Bimini Twist was my favorite restaurant. Mom and I only ate there on special occasions because it's a bit too expensive for us. Even though she worked directly for a CEO in Boca Raton, her Executive Assistant salary only went so far. As we entered the packed restaurant, Mechelle strode to the host to tell her we arrived for our reserved table. I scanned the restaurant, reminded of the many times' mom and I celebrated here.

Mechelle waved me over to follow her and the host to our table. We ambled past the bar area toward our tables. The large fish mounted on the wall at the back of the restaurant still there from when Mom and I had sat under it on her birthday.

We reached our booth; we perused the menu. Mechelle spent little time on it because she knew what she wanted. She and her family ate there frequently because they could afford it. It was her family's favorite as well. She peered at me with sad eyes, with pursed lips, "I've barely seen you since you came back from Kentucky." She pointed to the stone. "That's gorgeous. Is that the necklace you inherited from your grandmother?" she asked as she admired it.

"Yes, I can't remember a time when I didn't see her wearing it," I replied. We continued talking about Kentucky. She seemed interested in hearing more about Greg.

The server took our orders. I supplied her with more information about Greg and the Granaldis, making sure I did not disclose too much. I had been engrossed in our conversation; it shocked me to see our food arrive so quickly. The server placed my bowl of Seafood Pescatore with half a Lobster Tail in front of me. It looked like a piece of art. Beneath the lobster tail was a bed of linguine, with mussels, shrimp, scallops, and calamari tossed in a red seafood sauce. Among the many dishes I have tried, this was my favorite. Mechelle got the Blackened Ahi Tuna.

We finished our meal and strolled out to her car. I wanted a picture to remember this night. We snapped a selfie in front of the restaurant before she drove back to my house. I check the photo before texting it to Mechelle. Looking at the picture, a familiar man with dark hair stood in the background. I enlarged the photo to get a better view of him. I felt the hair on my arms rise and I gasped. I turned to Mechelle, "They're here. Why are they in Florida?" I could hear the panic in my voice. My heart started racing.

"Who's here?" she asked, sounding concerned.

"Those two guys following me in Louisville are here. They are in our photo. Well, one of them is." I looked through the rear window but did not notice them. *What should we do?* Caught up in my thoughts, I did not notice I was tapping on the phone. I showed her the picture at the first light. I scanned the area to see if they were following us.

I quickly called my mom and told her what had just happened, and she told me to come straight home. We did not see anyone following us, but it was dark and difficult to tell. Mechelle and I said our goodbyes in the car. Before exiting the car, I looked around, and I quickly made my way to my house. My mom must have been watching for me because she opened the door for me just as I was about to open it. Immediately she asked me if they followed me home. I assured her we did not see anyone following us. All I could think of was that I needed to talk to Phyllis. We never spoke before I left. I know my mother had informed her about our mysterious visitors.

My mom made me repeat everything I had told her over the phone. Moms' inquisition finally ended, and she headed to bed.

The graduation was at 8:00 am. The school required us there at 7:00 am, which meant I needed to be in bed. I entered my room, thinking about what a nice time I had tonight. At least until I discovered the Granaldi brothers. As I put my purse on my desk, it occurred to me I could not only speak to Phyllis, but I could also see her. I closed my blinds and locked my door before pulling the mirror from my purse. I opened the mirror and began concentrating on the kitchen of my grandmother's home. Before I knew it, the mirror pulls me in and suddenly I was on Grandma's kitchen floor.

Phyllis was not there. I thought for sure she would be there. I peeked out the window to see if her car was in the driveway. It was. Hurrying to the stairs, I noticed Greg's house through the window along the stairs.

"Ms. Phyllis, it's Brooke." She stuck her head through the doorway of my mother's room and seemed surprised to see me.

"Is everything okay?" she asked.

I told her about the Granaldis being in Florida and I showed her the picture, making sure I zoomed into the faces.

She looked closely at it and confirmed my suspicions. "It's the Granaldi brothers. You must try to avoid them. They are after the stone. They will continue to follow you and when you least expect it, they will attack. Your grandmother tried getting the police involved, but we felt like they have deep connections in law enforcement, which has kept them from being charged with anything. Eventually, the police stopped looking for them." She rubbed my arm and said, "I am proud of you for having the courage to use the stone on your own. That is something your grandmother would have done soon after receiving it." She told me, "You need to head home before your mother discovers you are missing."

I nodded and hugged her before opening the mirror and transported home. When I arrived, I checked my phone and saw that Greg had texted me. I did not hear the text when it initially came through.

GREG: I must miss you because I could have sworn, I just saw ya in your grandmother's foyer.

Realizing I need to be more careful when traveling, I texted him back.

BROOKE: Sorry to disappoint. I am still in Florida.

He must have seen me. I sent him my current location from my phone.

He texted a sad, emoji face.

I peered out my window to see if the Granaldi brothers were outside. There was only my mother's vehicle in sight.

The following morning, my mother came in to make sure I was getting ready. Feeling exhausted by everything, I was looking forward to my summer break. My mother brought me a small container of yogurt to eat while I continued dressing. Cooking had never been her thing. Growing up, she had a cook and never showed interest to learn. Our meals were mainly fast food or heating frozen dinners.

Eight

My mother had pressed my gown the night before and had it hanging on my closet door. I could not believe I am now a college student. *Goodbye, high school.* Those four years had flown by. I wondered; would college be the same way. I glanced at the clock and realized the time. I grabbed my cap and gown and asked Mom where her keys were.

Standing at the front door, she said, "I've got them. Are you ready to head out?"

I nodded. We both left the house, while I check to see if the Granaldi brothers were anywhere in sight. Relieved, they were not.

Once we arrive at the graduation ceremony, I searched for Mechelle and her family. My mother had planned to sit with them during the ceremony. After putting on my cap and gown, we strolled to the auditorium. Several friends and their families arrived at the same time. We acknowledged each other when Mechelle yells, "Brooke, over here."

I turned toward her voice and located Mechelle and her family. We all hugged one another, and Mechelle noticed I had my purse with me. She pointed to my purse and reminded me, "We can't have purses with us."

My mother said, "That's right." She motioned for me to hand her my purse. I nearly gave it to her when I remember the mirror. I took it from my purse and handed the purse to my mother.

Mechelle asked, "What's that?"

I told her it was my grandmother's and handed it to her.

Mechelle opened the mirror and took a quick peek at herself before closing and returning it to me. "It's beautiful. Your grandmother had great taste," she commented with a smile.

My mother told Mechelle's parents she would return in a minute because she wanted to lock my purse in the car.

Mechelle and I ambled to the entrance for the graduates, where they checked to make sure no one carried anything. I still had the mirror clutched in my hand when I realized they would not permit me entrance if I held it. My dress did not have pockets, so I did the next best thing and hid it in my bra.

Mechelle and I made our way through the line and checked in. Afterward, we met up with a few of our friends. We caught up with each other about what had been happening over the last few weeks.

We also talked about our plans after high school. Several of my friends were heading to college for the summer term. Like me, many were heading out-of-town the next day.

I couldn't believe it; we were ending this chapter of our lives.

Before lining up for the procession, we took group photos, with people's cell phones that had snuck them in. Mechelle took pictures of me with several of my favorite teachers and friends It was nice that they did not take the phones. Our principal announced it was time for us to line up and I found my spot between Brandon Gaffney and Gina Garrett. The music began playing from the other room. The line moved when Gina tapped me on the shoulder and said, "This is so exciting."

I smiled and continued following Brandon. All 824 seniors made it to their seats but remained standing while the National Anthem played. We sat. I tried locating my mother, but with so many people it would be impossible to locate her. We listened to a long list of speakers tell us about our accomplishments and to look toward our futures.

Finally, they began the Presentation of Candidates. I applauded everyone who crossed the stage. Ms. Peterson finally instructed us; the teacher assigned to our row to stand. We followed the line in front of us and made our way to the stage.

After receiving my diploma, I crossed the stage shaking everyone's hands. As I exited the stage, there was a photographer taking everyone's picture with their diploma. We continued making our way back to our seats. I looked at the diploma. This one paper shows validation of all my hard work.

Once the ceremony concluded, everyone made their way out of the building. My mom brought her pink umbrella to make it easier for Mechelle and me to locate her in the enormous crowd. As I exited, I was being pushed back and forth by the crowd. Many friends wished me good luck as we passed one another.

After the crowd thinned out, I searched for the pink umbrella. There were still too many people. I made my way farther away from the exit door and finally saw the umbrella. Mechelle had made it there before me. The five of us headed for brunch. Mom and I arrived before Mechelle and her family, so we waited at the table for them. Mr. and Mrs. Carpenter and Mechelle entered the restaurant. I waved at them.

The server came over for our drink order. I told Mechelle I was going to the restroom. The restroom was near the entrance to the restaurant. As I pushed the lady's room door open out of the corner of my eye, I spotted a familiar figure entering the restaurant. *Joseph Granaldi.*

We made eye contact, and I quickly made my way through the doorway. In a panic, I locked myself in the handicap stall. I used the restroom and listened for anyone else in the restroom. I heard no one. I washed and dried my hands in record time. The door to the ladies' room opened and shoes shuffled on the floor. The stone heated. I knew he was in the room. I looked under the door to confirm my suspicions.

Men's black sneakers.

I held my breath. My mind was going a thousand miles per minute as I tried to think of a way out of the situation. I knew he was about to make his move. *How do I get out of here?*

I remembered my mirror was still in my bra and I quickly pulled it out just as I heard the sound of what appeared to be the first stall door being pushed open.

In a straightforward and unemotional voice, I heard, "I know you're in here, Brooke. No one needs to get hurt. Give me the Bloom of Dreams and I will be on my way."

I was afraid to make a noise. The next stall door slammed open. In a stern gritty voice, "Don't make me break the door down. No one needs to get hurt."

I opened the mirror and wondered where I could go, but still, be close enough to return to my mother. Holding the mirror, I concentrated on the inside of my mother's car. Before I knew it, I was in the front passenger seat of my mother's vehicle.

I needed to return to the table. A car was parking across from me. Before exiting the car, I took another look around to make sure I did not see the Granaldis. The only people around me were the people exiting the vehicle in front of me. I scrambled out of the car, making sure I locked it. Made my way behind them as they made their way to the restaurant. Joseph exited the front door. He was on the phone and heading in the opposite direction. As soon as I could, I made a break for the front door and returned to my seat.

Sounding annoyed, my mother said, "Hurry and pick what you want. The server will be back in a minute to take our orders."

I decided on the crab eggs benedict. After we placed our order, Mrs. Carpenter turned to me and asked, "Where did you get that beautiful necklace? It looks remarkably like the star sapphire."

I reached up to touch the Bloom of Dreams, knowing I could not disclose the name of the stone. "This was my grandmother's necklace. I cannot think of a time she was not wearing it," I answered.

Mrs. Carpenter commented, "It's stunning."

While our parents talked about the changes occurring in our lives, Mechelle and I discussed Greg and Michael, the boy Mechelle had met when she went on a tour of her future school, Florida State University.

I could not help but wonder if the Granaldi brothers were waiting outside. We exited the restaurant; Mom and I gave the Carpenter's our goodbye hugs.

Just before Mechelle and I hugged goodbye, she asked, "Are you going to Samantha's party tonight."

Knowing Mom and I still had a few things to do before the morning and the Granaldis was near, I did not want to put anyone else in danger. I told her I could not make it.

During the ride home, Mom listed the things that still needed to be done before we headed back to Louisville. The moving company would be at our house between 1:00 pm and 3:00 pm. We stopped by the local storage company to pick up a few more boxes for the final few things that needed to be packed before heading home.

We were working hard cleaning and packing the last few things up for the movers. We were loading my mother's vehicle when they arrived. Before I knew it, the house was packed and on its way to Louisville. Mom and I looked around the house realizing it was really happening; we were entering a new chapter of our lives.

Knowing my mom really wanted to get back to Louisville to settle Grandma's estate. I turned to her and said, "It's only 7:30 pm. How about we start our trip to Kentucky now."

I could see the shock in my mother's face at my suggestion. She asked, "We're done early, are you sure you don't want to go to Samantha's party?"

"I'm excited about our new adventure. Let's head out," I said with a smile and grateful I was with my mother in case the Granaldis showed up. I must admit, I was looking forward to seeing Greg also.

"Let me give the key to Susie before we go," she said as she started taking the house key off the key chain to give to our next-door neighbor. Susie was also a member of our church.

My key was in the lockbox for the realtor.

She added, "Please text Maryanne and tell her Susie has our house key. Maryanne and her sons are picking up the furniture and things from the house. She will be providing them to a Lake Worth family in need."

While I texted Maryanne, Mom headed next door to give Susie the key. I explored the house to make sure nothing was forgotten.

Mom returned and asked, "Are you ready to go?"

I glanced around to get one last look at our home and nodded. As my mother locked the door, I realized this chapter of my life was officially over. We pulled out of the driveway, and I texted Greg to let him know we are on our way to Louisville. He texted me back a smiley face emoji. We drove for several hours before stopping in Leesburg for the night because of exhaustion. We went straight to bed.

Nine

My mother's annoying cell phone alarm woke me. I rolled over, trying to focus on the clock. I could not believe it was already 5:30 am. *Does she not hear that?* The alarm continued to rattle my nerves. "Mom…. Mom… Mom." As I raised my voice, she still did not stir. Clinching the pillow in my hand, I tossed it at her head. *Wow, great aim, Brooke.*

She finally rolled over, glared at me, before announcing in a very groggy morning voice, "I don't want to get up."

I grinned, "Come on, we need to get going. I'll drive so you can get some more sleep." I dressed quickly, packed, and grabbed the car keys before heading to the car to put my suitcase in the trunk. Passing through the lobby, I spotted the complimentary coffee and grabbed us both a cup before hurrying to the room. I gently kicked the door to let my mother know I was outside, but no answer. *Perhaps she is not up.* Trying not to spill the coffee, I kicked a little harder.

She pulled the door open as she adjusted her shirt. She grabbed the coffee, savored it, and smirked, "You are so good to me."

Once Mom finished packing, I did a walk-through to make sure we left nothing in the room. As I walked to the parking lot, I wondered if the Granaldi brothers would follow us back to Kentucky. This made me feel as though I could not breathe. I stopped at McDonald's for breakfast, but Mom slept through it. I left her breakfast in the bag for when she woke up, which did not happen until we reached Valdosta, Georgia.

She slowly woke up, stretched her arms and legs out, "I can't believe how tired I was."

"We've been through a lot the past few weeks. It's drained us both. I went to McDonald's and grabbed you a sausage biscuit and a bottle of water," I said as I motioned toward the bag.

She ate, while I concentrated on the road. Mom turned the radio up. We only had two more miles until the next rest stop. Mom finished her breakfast and collected the trash. I flipped my blinker on to head to the rest stop, Mom quickly put her shoes on. I parked the car, and we both headed to the restroom.

When we exited the restroom, Mom reached out her hand, "I'll drive."

I handed her the keys and looked around at how different Georgia was from South Florida. It was so beautiful. As we approached our car, I noticed Tony Granaldi smoking a cigarette. He was about ten cars from ours, "Mom, look ahead."

She looked in his direction, swung the car door open. "Quick, get in the car."

As Mom pulled out, I watched to see if they were following us. He stood there smoking his cigarette, it seemed as if he searched for someone. Near the restrooms, the other brother stood in front of the vending machine.

"Mom let's get off at the next exit before they catch us. We can let them continue north while we wait so we can monitor them," I instructed.

"That's a great idea," she said, as she pressed the accelerator.

It was not like Mom to speed, but I think she was as concerned as I was about the Granaldi brothers. I wished I could have told her why they were following us, but I knew I should not. I kept a watch for their car, which I believed was a black Toyota Camry. She flicked the blinker on right before she exited I-75. Mom turned right to head toward the major businesses. We pulled into a gas station. Going to the pumps on the backside to help prevent them from finding us. While Mom pumped gas, I continued looking for their car. She went into the store and returned with a bag.

"I got us some snacks," she said, as she settled back into the driver's seat.

I looked through the bag. There were a few bottles of water, a bag of Doritos, two Snickers, and a bag of Peanut M&Ms. We waited about ten more minutes before we headed back to I-75.

"Mom, I can't tell you how many black Toyota Camrys we passed since we saw them, but it's a lot," I said, as Mom switched lanes. "It's going to be hard to find them."

Mechelle texted me pictures from graduation and Samantha's party. I flipped through them and realized I should have gone to the party. The last picture was of Samantha and Mechelle holding a sign that said, "We Miss You." I sent her a smiling emoji and a text saying, "I miss you too."

We stopped several more times for gas, lunch, and dinner, bathroom breaks, and to switch drivers. Fortunately, we never saw the Granaldi brothers. It was nearly 9:30 pm when we pulled into the driveway, and that is when it hit me. This was our new home. I needed to stop referring to it as my grandmother's house. We parked the car and Phyllis came out the back door to greet us.

"Are you ladies hungry?" she asked.

I gave her a big hug, "I could use a snack."

Mom popped the trunk, and I pulled the first suitcase out.

Greg came walking down our driveway, "How was the trip?" He grabbed the other suitcase from the trunk. It was so nice to see him. The butterflies in my stomach stirred.

I started telling him about the Granaldi brothers being in Florida, as he picked up the suitcase from the ground and motioned with his head for me to go ahead of him. I quickly opened the back door to let him in.

He asked," Where do these go?"

"You're so sweet. The blue one is mine. Just leave it in the hall on the second floor. The black one is my mother's. It needs to go to the third-floor. Mom has moved to my grandmother's room. Ya know, the one we boxed all the clothes in," I said with a smile.

Greg nodded and made his way upstairs. I put my purse on the desk in the hall before heading back to the kitchen to join Phyllis and my mother. My mom was sitting at the counter eating a bowl of fruit salad.

Phyllis handed me two bowls of the salad, "There are waters for you and Greg on the counter."

I took the bowls to the dining room and returned for napkins, silverware, and the bottled waters before returning to the dining room. Greg came into the dining room to join me. We discussed the last few days, including the trip back home.

"My Grandmother never had a Wi-Fi setup. Mom still needs to get it. Do ya have Wi-Fi I could use to research the Granaldi family? I'm hoping to find information about them." I said as I popped a grape in my mouth.

Greg took a swig of water, "Sure. Just let me know when you want to come over."

Mom and Phyllis joined us. Phyllis informed us she moved her bedroom to the second floor. She okayed this with my mother while we were in Florida. I know that made me happy because it would be easier for her and me to keep things from Mom if we were on the same floor. Mom excused herself and headed to bed.

Greg stood, "I should head out too. I'll let myself out. Have a good night."

Phyllis and I sat and chatted about her sister for a few minutes before I headed to bed.

Ten

Waking to the singing of a bird outside my window, I rolled over to see if I could see the bird. The sun shining through the curtain was bright. The bird was out of sight. I threw on sweats before heading downstairs. As I hit the bottom of the staircase, it sounded like someone was in the kitchen. I noticed Greg's truck in his driveway as I looked out the foyer window. When I entered the kitchen, Phyllis was making waffles for breakfast. The aroma of chocolate filled the air, "Those smell wonderful."

"I made chocolate waffles for you today," Phyllis informed me as she pulled the waffle from the waffle iron and put it on the plate next to another one. She added powdered sugar on the waffles and fruit salad from last night next to them on the plate. She placed the plate and a fork on the counter by the stool. I made myself a cup of coffee before sitting and eating my breakfast. "Do you think we could visit another place today?" I asked.

Phyllis was cleaning up the kitchen. "With the Granaldi brothers following you, you need to become more familiar with the stone. We need to make sure we are incredibly careful when traveling because no one must discover the secrets of it." She took my empty plate. I headed out to the car and unloaded our boxes and to get our computers inside. I left mine on the desk in the foyer and brought my mother's upstairs and put it on the table in the hall, making sure I did not wake her. I took several boxes that contained mementos from our childhoods and placed them in the garage until we knew where we were to put them. I placed the remaining boxes in the foyer for my mother to sort through before grabbing a box for my room.

I entered my room, put a box of my things on the table by the high-back chairs. Ripping the tape off the box and opened it. The first thing I noticed was the picture of my father and me. We were on a carousel at Disney World. I was sitting on a horse and my father stood with his arm wrapped around me. My parents had taken me there for my tenth birthday. Soon after this trip, my parents divorced. My father was not around much. Even less after the divorce. I would love to say not having him around was difficult, but it was easier because his drinking was out of control.

When I was about twelve, I noticed he was drinking a lot. He always had alcohol on his breath. I will never forget; I was fourteen when he died. It was Super Bowl Sunday. He had too much to drink, ran off the road right into a tree. They rushed him to the hospital, but he died on the way.

I put the picture of us on my dresser and unpacked the other items in the box. My phone vibrated to let me know I received a text.

GREG: Come over whenever you want to use our Wi-Fi.

I texted back.

BROOKE: I will be over in a few minutes.

Continuing to unpack the clothes that were still in the box before bringing the box downstairs. The boxes were left in the foyer in case my mother wanted to pack more of Grandma's things up. I grabbed my computer and told Phyllis where I was going before heading to Greg's home.

He answered the door and let me in. The design style differed greatly from my new home. His home had a more rustic farmhouse feel. The living room had a beige sofa with beige and blue throw pillows and two beige accent chairs. The coffee table was rustic with several colors of paints that gave it an aged look. There was a windowpane hung above the sofa like a piece of art. Greg led me into his dining room, just off the kitchen. A white wooden table with black wooden chairs took up much of the room. A black iron chandelier above the table was something one would find in a farmhouse. I sat down at the table and Greg handed me a piece of paper with the Wi-Fi information. I set up the Wi-Fi, as Karen came in. She was still in her pajamas and looked as though she had just crawled out of bed. She kind of waved at me as she headed into the kitchen. Greg sat next to me. I pulled my pen and paper out of my bag and searched the internet for anything that could help us.

It did not take long. "Anthony Granaldi III has two sons, Anthony "Tony" Granaldi IV and Joseph Granaldi. The Granaldi brother's father is still alive and resides in Italy. They are part of a mafia and believed to have police officers in prominent positions on their payroll," I said, with concern.

"That must be why they never get caught," Greg said.

"At least I could find some information." *I need to go there and see what I can find out about Mr. Anthony Granaldi III.* I closed my computer and started packing up my things when someone came in the front door. A lady entered the dining-room from the kitchen dressed in a wet t-shirt, stretchy pants, and sneakers.

"You must be Brooke. I'm sorry for your loss. I'm Joann, Greg's mom. You must forgive me, there's a group of us that goes walking every morning and I'm in desperate need of a shower." She pivoted toward the doorway.

"It's nice to meet you," I said, hoping she heard me. Grabbing my things, "Thank you for letting me come over." I said as I started heading to his front door. Greg walked me home. He is such a gentleman. *How did I get so lucky?* Exiting his home, I scanned the road for the black Camry. The Granaldis were nowhere in sight. I thanked him again and headed into the house. Upon opening the front door, I found Mom at the desk on the phone and Phyllis polishing the furniture in the drawing-room.

With Mom being busy, I tested out the stone in my room. Phyllis said the stone could make me invisible. I looked into my full-length mirror and pictured myself in the drawing-room, invisible. The drawing-room became visible in the mirror, and I stepped into it. Glancing down at my hands to confirm I was invisible; I found my hands before me. *What did I do wrong?* Feeling disappointed, I looked at the mirror behind the bar for my reflection to see if I looked any different, but I could not see my reflection. I had done it; I was invisible!

Phyllis made her way over to polish the bar. I tiptoed over and stood on the other side of the bar to see if she could see me. She did not seem to notice me. I muttered, "Phyllis, I'm in front of you."

Phyllis looked up with a puzzled look and whispered, "Brooke?"

I whispered back, "I figured out how to make myself invisible."

From the foyer, mom hollered, "Phyllis did you say something?"

Phyllis's eyes got big. "No ma'am," Phyllis said to Mom before whispering to me, "Go before we get caught."

Remembering my compact mirror was in my purse upstairs, I snuck past Mom and up the stairs. I went straight to my mirror in my room. I stared into the full-length mirror and pictured myself visible in my room. My room appeared in the mirror, and I stepped through it, which brought me back to where I was standing, but I was facing the opposite direction. I headed downstairs to see if my mother was off the phone. She was. Some boxes were open. She must have unpacked.

"I am glad you came back down. The police officer I spoke to about the Granaldis, could not locate the two men that are following us. I told him they had been in Florida, but he said the trail here was cold. I just cannot imagine what they are looking for. Mr. Thomas and I have discussed it and we can't figure out what they want. Whatever it is, we should get rid of it, so they leave us alone," she said, before opening a large box.

Thankfully, she does not know what they want. I must protect the Bloom of Dreams at all costs. We finished unpacking the boxes, and I took the empty boxes out to the garage. As I was looking around at the things Grandma had in her garage, Greg texted.

GREG: Are you interested in going to a bonfire at my buddy Austin's house tonight?

I went inside and asked my mother if she was okay with me going. She said, "I'm glad you are making friends already. Yes, you may go, but don't be out too late and make sure you stay with Greg. With those men following us, we need to be extra careful."

Shocked, she was letting me go. "I won't be out late, and I will make sure I stay with Greg," I headed up to my room, grabbed my speaker, and brought it outside with me to the balcony. I turned country music on and sat down on the sofa and texted Greg.

BROOKE: I can go, but I can't be out late. What time?

GREG: They are having BBQ chicken for dinner. I'll pick you up at 6:30 pm.

I ran downstairs. Mom was in the kitchen with Phyllis making lunch. "Mom, Greg said they are having a BBQ also," I said, with excitement about going out with Greg.

Phyllis said, "I will make mini pineapple upside-down cakes for you to take with you tonight."

"Ms. Phyllis, how do you have time to do so much? You have more energy than most people.", I said, amazed by her.

"I've taken care of this home for so long; I have had plenty of practice to work out the best routine to get things done quickly and efficiently. It doesn't hurt that I love baking," she giggled.

After enjoying a scrumptious chef salad for lunch and a great conversation with Phyllis and Mom, I headed up to my room to figure out what I had to wear since most of my wardrobe was on the moving truck. I decided on jeans, a pink tank top, and a blue and pink sweater with brown ankle boots. I laid the clothes on my bed and changed into my bathing suit to get some sun before getting ready. I grabbed a towel, my phone, my speaker, and the mirror. I made my way to the third-floor balcony because it received direct sunlight, unlike the balcony in my room.

I laid in the chaise lounge thinking about my grandmother. *What did she see in me to bestow such a gift?* We have distant cousins she could have chosen. I wondered if they knew about the stone. Never met them, not even sure how well they knew my grandmother or if they even knew her at all. I looked down at the stone. *Are you a blessing or a curse?*

The Granaldi brothers came to mind. *How can I protect myself from them?* I created a list in my head of skills I might need to defend myself. Although they had not attacked, the Granaldi brothers are dangerous. After learning more about their family, it is more important than ever I learned how to protect myself. *There must be somewhere here to take self-defense classes, or I could take taekwondo or karate. Oh, there's kickboxing too.* I had so many options, but whatever I decide I needed to act soon.

Spying would hone my skills, and I could find out more about the Granaldis. I cannot just go spy on them. I need to practice first. It occurred to me I could spy on Greg if he were at home. I ran down to my balcony to see if his truck was at his house.

I had a full view of their driveway and back yard. Karen, Greg, and another guy were sitting in the backyard. Before starting my spy mission, I returned to my room, and slid the compact mirror inside my bathing suit. Standing in front of the full-length mirror, I encourage myself to be brave and have the courage to be fearless and step into the full-length mirror. I concentrated on Greg's backyard and me being invisible, picturing them sitting at his patio table.

As I stepped through the mirror, I gently stepped into Greg's backyard. Finding myself about seven feet away from the table, I did not move out of fear of being discovered. Greg and the mystery man talked about trucks. Karen sat next to our mystery man playing on her phone. The mystery man was thin and had thick blond hair a little longer than Greg's. His cheeks and nose were covered in freckles.

Greg turned to Karen, "What time is it?"

Karen looked annoyed that she had to stop what she was doing to check the time. She switched screens and jumped out of her chair. "It's 4:30. I need to get my toes done, she said before rushing into the house."

"So, what's the deal, man?" the mystery guy asked.

Looking confused, Greg said, "What do ya mean?"

"Karen tells me you have a date tonight," he inquired.

Just as Greg was about to answer, Joann walked through the French doors that led to the backyard. "Hello, Travis," she said with a smile.

"Hello, Mrs. Scrogham," Travis answered.

"Gregory, Karen said she is going with you tonight to Austin's party. Is that correct?" she inquired.

"I guess," he said, sounding disappointed.

"Mrs. Scrogham, I was thinking I would take her and let Greg be able to take his date without his sister in the car. Is that okay?" he asked, and I could tell Greg seemed pleased.

Joann looked at Travis and back at Greg, who looked at his mother. After a long pause, she said to Travis, "That's fine, but make sure she knows your intentions. All I need around here is her thinking it's a date." She headed back into the house.

After making sure the door was closed, Travis turned to Greg and asked, "Are ya going to spill the beans?"

Greg tried to hold back his smile, "Brooke just moved in next door. We met when she came up for her grandmother's funeral. She's pretty cool and oddly mysterious."

"Mysterious?" he asked.

"Ya," he said and leaned closer to Travis. "There's been some strange things going on since her grandma died. There are people following them. They think they are the same people that attacked their attorney and stole her grandma's will," he added before leaning back in his chair.

A bee buzzed near my ear. I backed up, trying not to get stung. "Clank", Oh no, I backed right into the grill.

Greg and Travis looked in my direction. "Did ya hear that?" Travis asked Greg.

"Ya," he said as he started heading in the grill's direction. "There has got to be a critter in the grill."

Oh no, I need to get out of here. I stepped away from the grill and onto the lawn. As I backed up, I noticed I was making footprints in the grass. Feeling my pulse race, I opened the mirror and concentrated on the third-floor balcony. I was flung out of the mirror onto the balcony; I realized I really enjoy using items I can walk into, or I needed to figure out how to land on my feet. I grabbed my things and headed back to my room. I heard water coming from my bathroom; I walked in, and Phyllis was cleaning the sink.

"Where have you been hiding out?" Phyllis asked as she grabbed my laundry.

Feeling guilty for spying on Greg. "I was on the third-floor balcony getting some sun," I followed her out of my bathroom and as she walked to the doorway I asked, "Do you know how Grandma could come out of the mirror and land on her feet?"

"No, I'm afraid not, but perhaps you should concentrate on landing on your feet," she said before heading downstairs.

I closed my bedroom door and went to the bathroom for a shower.

Eleven

The guilt from spying on Greg was stirring emotions in me I had never felt for a boy. I cared about him. *He must never find out or it could destroy our friendship. I must figure out another way to practice spying without feeling like I am intruding on someone's privacy.* Excited about the evening, I stepped out of the shower and dried myself off. After wiping the steam off the mirror with a towel, I touched my sunburned nose. I put my robe on and dried my hair before putting my makeup on and dressing. With about thirty minutes to spare, I went to the library to see if my grandmother had left me hidden secrets about the stone. She read to me from the many books as a young child.

I found a childhood favorite, The Story of Doctor Dolittle, and smiled, remembering my grandmother reading to me. The cover showed Doolittle surrounded by monkeys in a forest. It appeared they were about to eat a meal. Opening the book, I discovered they published it in 1920. I wonder how many of my ancestors had read this book.

Returning it to the shelf. I need to search for books that might help me with the Bloom of Dreams. Not knowing where to start my search, I started strolling along the bookshelves to see if something caught my eye. Phyllis had been so helpful in leading me in the right direction, but I wished my grandmother could have answered my questions.

I discovered there were many books on various topics: Engineering, medicine, surgery, non-fiction, fiction, biographies, travel books... Oddly, there is such a variety. The doorbell chimes rang, Greg had arrived. I headed downstairs to find Mom and Greg talking about where we were going. He gazed up at me, smiled, and his cheeks became pink. *Is he blushing?* I tried to hold back a smile. I could feel the adrenaline start rushing through me. I was so excited about the evening. He was checking me out. I must admit, I was checking him out too. The butterflies were back in my stomach. He had on much nicer boots than the ones I have seen him wearing, which matched well with his navy-blue t-shirt underneath a navy blue and white plaid shirt. He had even gotten a haircut.

"You look beautiful," he announced as he looked over me.

Wanting to compliment him, but not finding the words, I muttered, "Thank you."

Greg turned to my mother, "What time should she be home?" Mom looked at both of us, "11:30 pm, sharp."

Phyllis walked out with the mini pineapple upside-down cakes for the BBQ. I thanked her for them and took them before heading to the front door. He walked me to his truck, which was parked out front. As we approached the black iron gate, he politely opened it and let me exit before shutting it behind him. He opened the passenger door, which was when I got a whiff of his cologne. He took the cakes and put them in the back seat behind me. Once I was in my seat, he closed the door and walked around to the driver's side. He started the truck and pulled out and headed toward Austin's house. The Granaldis, losing my grandmother, the stress of the move, seemed unimportant. Euphoria is the best way I could describe what I was feeling. I never looked out the window to see if the Granaldi's were following us, I was not worried about helping Mom, or even thinking about the Bloom of Dreams. I just sat there thinking about the smell of his cologne, fresh and clean. It was not musky like some men's colognes. If there was such a thing as a love potion, I think this is what it would smell like.

Greg gazed at me for a moment, "You're going to meet some of my friends tonight. Austin and I have been friends since third grade. I don't think anyone knows me better than him. His family is farmers, and we will always have each other's backs. We've been through a lot together over the years. My buddy, Zack, will be there too. He's fun to hang out with, but he is a big flirt. Travis is going to bring my sister. They're not dating, but she's coming to hang out with Austin's sister Lisa."

We had been driving for a while down Bardstown Road before getting off at the Mount Washington exit. It occurred to me that Greg must be from the area. We continued on a country road for several miles before we turned right onto a dirt road. We passed an extensive cornfield, turned left on another dirt road that appeared to be a driveway.

The house had red bricks and black shutters. A single white door was surrounded by a small porch on the modest home. Several trucks and a few cars parked along the drive. Greg drove toward the house, turned the truck around, and headed back up the drive before parking. He got out and walked around the truck to open my door. Not one boy in Florida ever did this for me.

He reached out his hand to help me out of the vehicle. I grabbed his hand. It felt warm to the touch. I did not want to release him. He opened the back door and grabbed the mini pineapple upside-down cakes. We went straight to the backyard.

As we approached, I could hear Blake Shelton's "God's Country" playing. Several people sat at a picnic table, and a few guys were setting up the bonfire. One of them was Travis. Greg faced me and said, "I'll be right back." He headed to the table filled with desserts. He placed the cakes with the other desserts. Greg led me to the fire pit area. I looked around for Karen. She was not around.

One guy with blond curly hair and a pretty bad sunburn, turned around and said, "Hey man, long time no see. Where ya been?" He looked me over.

He had a strong southern accent. Greg had one too, but not as bad.

Greg said, "I've been working on my truck. This is Brooke. Brooke, this is Austin."

"Thank you for having me," I said.

After placing another log on the pile, the huskier boy with brown wavy hair left the others and headed our way. Patting Greg on the back. He pivoted toward me and said, "Well, who are you, my fair lady?" He bowed.

My guess, this was Zack.

"This is Brooke. Brooke, Zack," he said, as he moved his head toward Zack.

"If you need anything, my fair lady, Zack is here to serve you," he bowed again and joined his other friends.

The man standing at the grill announced, "Gather around everyone, dinner is ready." He took the last few pieces of chicken off the grill and took the plate of chicken to the table with all the other food before turning around. "Please bow your heads," he said, as he looked around before speaking, "Our Father in heaven, thank you for this land and our harvest. We give thanks for this food and the hands that prepared it for the nourishment of our bodies. We pray for our crops, the health of our family and friends. In the name of Jesus, we pray. Amen," he said before stepping aside for everyone to be able to get food.

Austin resembled him. Greg and I walked toward the line for food. Karen and another girl about her age were pouring drinks for everyone. She must be Lisa. The lady making sure everything was on the table was probably Austin's mother. She was a little overweight had light brown hair in a bob. Greg motioned for me to go before him in the line. I grabbed a plate, fork, and knife, and made my way down the line. I took a piece of chicken, baked beans, mac-n-cheese, corn on the cob, and a piece of cornbread.

As we approached the drink table, Karen filled a cup with iced tea, "Hey Brooke, what would you like to drink?"

I looked at the choices on the table, sweet tea, lemonade, coke, water, or big red. I informed her I wanted lemonade. Karen poured my drink. While I grabbed my drink, Karen's friend poured Greg sweet tea. I stepped away from the table. Greg led me to the picnic table where there were still a few seats left.

Greg said, "Hey guys, make some room."

Everyone at the table looked up. Austin and Travis made room for us. I sat between Austin and Greg. Once we settled into our seats, Travis leaned forward and looked my way before saying, "Hey Brooke, I'm Travis."

I smiled, "Hello." I was feeling rather shy because I only knew Greg and Karen, and Karen was sitting with her friend in the chairs surrounding the fire pit. Greg and his friends talked about the work Greg had done on his truck while I ate. The baked beans reminded me of Phyllis's beans. They were thick and I could taste the brown sugar. I took a bite of the mac-n-cheese. *Wow, they are so creamy. So much better than the boxed mac-n-cheese Mom and I always eat.*

Greg turned to me, "How's the food?"

"It's delicious," I said as I took my first bite of the chicken. I have never tasted a barbecue sauce like this. "Do you know what kind of BBQ sauce this is? It's amazing," I asked before taking a second bite.

"Bill makes his sauce," Greg informed me before taking a bite of his chicken.

During a break in the conversation, I asked about his farm.

With great pride, he informed me, "This farm has been in my family for years. My great-grandfather purchased the farm. Farming can be a rough life, but I love it," he concluded as his dad came and patted him on the back.

"Don't be bashful guys, there is plenty more food," Bill said before noticing me.

As I focused on Bill, I noticed his curly blond hair was greying. He was a large muscular man with a farmer's tan and wore a short sleeve green t-shirt with a tractor and the words, "Support Your Local Farmers."

"How are ya little lady?" he asked.

I smiled, "I'm Brooke. I'm here with Greg," I reached out to shake his hand. "This barbecue is amazing. Greg said you make it yourself," I said.

"Well, thank you, that is my Western Kentucky barbecue. I took my dad's sauce, made a few changes, and this is the result," Bill informed me. "Enjoy," he said, as he moved on.

I finished my dinner, while Greg talked to Zack. I made eye contact with Austin, "Greg said he has known you most of his life."

Austin finished chewing his food and said, "Yah, we are like brothers. We've each other's backs. He's always been there for me and my family. A few years back, he missed a few weeks of school helping us on the farm because dad broke his arm. We can't afford to lose a man when it's time to harvest our crops. He attended summer school to make up the work to remain on track. That's a genuine friend."

"That is amazing," I glanced over at Greg, realizing he is even more extraordinary than I thought.

Greg stood up and asked me, "What would you like for dessert?" I went to get up, and he grabbed my plate, "I got it."

The table was filled with a lemon cake, an apple pie, the mini pineapple upside down cakes, and chocolate chip cookies. "A small piece of lemon cake and a mini pineapple upside down cake," I answered.

Austin and I continued our conversation. "He's a great guy. Please don't break his heart," Austin warned.

My facial expression probably showed how surprised I was by his comment. "I don't plan on hurting him. We just met, but from what I know about him so far is he is a spectacular guy. He's been nothing but a gentleman to me. From the moment I met him, he has been helpful to my mom and me. He seems to be trustworthy, loyal, and a helpful friend," I informed him.

Greg returned with our desserts and with Austin's mother. He placed my plate in front of me before placing his plate on the table and sat next to me.

"Brooke, we are glad to have you with us today. Did you get enough to eat?" Austin's mother asked.

"I did, thank you. Everything was delicious," I said.

"Thank you for the pineapple upside-down cakes. They were delicious," she said. "I'm Lisa. Let me know if ya need anything."

"I will let Phyllis know you like them," I answered, not realizing she did not know who Phyllis was, but could not explain before she went to Karen. We finished dessert and excused ourselves from the table.

Greg had me follow him to a horseshoe pit. He reached down and picked up the horseshoes. He handed me the red ones, and he took the blue ones. "Have you played?" he asked.

"Yes, but I am not very good," I said as I lined up to throw the horseshoe. My first one landed nowhere near the stake. I looked up at Greg. He was holding back a smirk. Taking a deep breath and slowly exhaling, I tossed the second horseshoe. It landed right next to the stake but did not hit it. I turned to Greg and smiled.

"It looks like I might have some competition," he said as he prepared to throw his first horseshoe. He lined himself up and seemed so focused. I watched him toss it and it was a ringer. He threw his second horseshoe, and it was also a ringer.

"Six points, you're good," I said as we walked to get our horseshoes.

"Austin and I have spent many hours here playing," he said.

We continued playing until Greg won twenty-one to six. I am pretty sure he let me have those six points.

Zack and Travis wanted to play. We moved out of the way for them. We watched them as they played. When they finished, it was too dark for another game.

Austin came over and said, "Guys, Dad wants us to light the fire."

We hurried over to the fire pit and watched as Austin lit the fire. We hung out around the fire for a while, talking and eating s'mores.

Twelve

Greg wanted to go for a walk. It excited me we would have some alone time. We ambled away from the house along a pathway covered with a canopy from the maple trees. We took a left, bringing us to the barn. He took me to a swing for two. It hung from a maple tree next to the barn. We both sat and gently swung. The crickets sounded off in the distance and lightning bugs lit just above the grass.

I turned to Greg, "Look! Lightning bugs." I jumped up. "We don't have lightning bugs in south Florida," He watched me trying to catch one.

Large hairy arms grabbed me from behind and pulled me toward the barn, "I've got you now. You'll give me the necklace," he said, as he was pulling me toward the other side of the barn. The necklace was hot. I must not have felt the stone warming because I was bent over trying to catch the lightning bugs as it dangled away from my skin.

Greg ran toward us. While turning toward the assailant he turned flinging his leg in the air barely missing my head and hitting my assailant. As we both fell to the ground, the hairy arms released their grip on me. I darted away from him, moving a few feet behind Greg. *Joseph Granaldi.* Joseph was trying to recover from the kick to his head. He was on his knees, when Greg kicked him across the chest, knocking him to the ground.

"Come on," Greg grabbed my hand and led me toward the cornfield. Tony came from the other direction. The nearly full moon lit the pathway, so we could see well. The leaves of the cornstalks brushed against me as we sprinted through the field. Greg shifted directions frequently. On one turn, I fell to the ground. Greg helped me up and Tony headed straight for us with a pistol in his hand.

He fired his gun in our direction but missed us.

We turned right into another row. We exited that row and ran down another pathway. I could not believe the Granaldi's would attempt to kill me. *I cannot let Greg get hurt because of me.* My mirror was in my purse in Greg's truck.

Greg pulled me to the right. I pulled back because the pond was in front of us. "No, this way." I pulled him in the pond's direction. I knew I could not let him get hurt.

"We are in the open. We need to hide," he said, trying to pull me toward the cornfields.

The Granaldi brothers shooting in our direction. The bullets nearly hit us as they struck the ground and water around us.

The water! Without my mirror, I could use the water. "Trust me," I focused on the water and pictured my room. I grabbed his arm and pulled him behind me.

The stone flung us out of the mirror. When he realized where we were he looked around in amazement. His face told me he was in shock and confused.

"What? How?" he asked looking frantically around the room.

I gently shut the door. Placing my finger on my mouth. He needed to be quiet, and I need to think. *What should we do?* I felt sick thinking about the others we left there with those men.

"Brooke, what just happened? How did we get here? Those guys were shooting at us and why aren't we wet?" he asked, as he examined his clothes.

I had not realized we never got wet, but I knew he deserved an explanation. "I'm going to confide something in you. You can't tell another soul. Those men have been after my family for the Bloom of Dreams. It was what I used to teleport from the field here. It saved our lives."

"We need to get back and warn everyone. Karen, she is still there too," he said, with a worried look on his face.

"Okay, we can't let anyone see us when we return," I grabbed his hand to move us back in front of my full-length mirror. I instructed him to hold my arm, which he did. I gazed into the mirror and envisioned us in his truck.

The image appeared and Greg looked at me more confused than ever. I entered the mirror, pulling him behind me. Squatted down to make sure we would fit in the cab. I made my way to my seat and Greg followed me and got in his.

"That's amazing. Am I dreaming?" he said before looking around.

I caught myself biting my lip. Grabbing Greg's arm," Wait. No, you're not dreaming."

I grabbed my mirror from my purse and slipped it into my pocket, and we sneaked out of the truck and back to the backyard. The music played and people talked. Austin, Lisa, Karen, and his parents were taking the food in the house. We pursued them.

"Greg, where have you both been? We heard some gunfire and got concerned," Lisa asked.

"We were down at the barn and some man grabbed Brooke. I fought him off, and we ran through the cornfields to get a way. As we were getting away, he fired his gun at us."

In shock, Lisa said, "Bill, we must call the police!"

"Boys, get everyone in the house immediately. Girls close all the blinds and kill the lights," he said as he dialed 911.

We joined the others in the other room on the floor. I could barely hear Bill on the phone because everyone raised their voices trying to figure out what was going on. Without notice, Bill whistled. "Be quiet and someone shut that radio off!" he yelled before returning to the call.

I could hear him repeating the address to the person on the other end of the phone. When he got off the phone, he left the room and came back with a shotgun.

Bill looked out the windows. I started thinking about how I had put everyone in danger. I can only imagine what was going through Greg's head about everything happening. We finally heard sirens coming from the distance. Greg must have noticed how worried I was because he reached down and grabbed my hand. It was so comforting. *I sure hope I can trust him to keep my secret.* All the excitement of the event and concern for the danger I have put everyone in was making me nauseous.

The sirens became louder, and the lights flashed red and blue through the curtains. Bill went out to talk to the officers out front, and I could not make out anything they were saying.

Greg got up and reached out his hand to help me up. We waited inside for either Bill or the deputy to instruct us otherwise. They were out there for a while. A helicopter circled above the house. Finally, Bill and the deputy came into the house. Bill told Greg and me to go to the kitchen. The officer took our statements and handed us a few papers to complete, while he went back outside. Greg and I completed the paperwork, and we waited for the officer to return.

Lisa entered the kitchen. "How are you doing, sweetie?" she asked while stroking her hand down my head in the way a mother would with her child.

"I'm a little shook up. Why do ya think he attacked me?" I looked at her, I knew she would not know the real reason.

"I'm not sure, darlin', but there has been a lot in the news about human trafficking. Greg and Austin should teach you karate so you can defend yourself," she said, looking over at Greg.

I shot him a look. "That's how you could break me free," I stated.

He smiled at me. "I'm just glad you're safe." Greg grabbed my hand and gave it a gentle squeeze.

The front door opened again, and the officer and Bill walked into the kitchen. The officer picked up our completed paperwork from the table. After looking over the paperwork, "Well, we found the rounds shot off, but it looks like they got away. We found footprints that led to the edge of the property. We will let you know if we find anything else out. Oddly, it looks like we tracked your tracks to the pond, but we lost them." He paused before saying goodbye and heading out.

I had totally lost track of the time and looked at my phone, surprised it was nearly 11:00 pm. It took us about thirty minutes to get there. I showed Greg my phone, and he headed to the other room.

His friends started asking all kinds of questions, but Greg interrupted them, "We'll talk later. We need to get home."

We said our goodbyes quickly before leaving.

On the way home, Karen could not stop asking questions. Concerned they might have tried to get her caused her to panic. She was thankful she stayed at the house. I found myself half-listening to her. My mind was on Greg. *What is he thinking? Will he keep my secret? How am I going to explain what happened?* I so desperately needed to explain everything to Greg.

Greg made sure I arrived home on time. We pulled in front of my house at 11:27 pm. Karen stayed in his truck while he walked me to the door. "Can you do me a favor? Would you come talk to me when your mom thinks you are in bed?" he asked.

I know he wants answers. I can't blame him, "I will try. Where do you want me to meet you?"

"How about at my truck?" he asked.

"Okay, but if I'm not there by 12:30 am, I won't be able to make it," I headed into the house.

It appeared no one was downstairs. I locked the door and headed upstairs. Phyllis had her door open, so I knocked on the door frame.

"How was your date?" she asked, with a smile.

I filled her in on everything that occurred.

"You've had a lot on your plate. You were right to reveal your secret to save your lives, and in doing you also protected the stone. Lillie would be proud. I will tell your mother the story you gave to the police. She went to bed early. Her plan is to check out a church in the morning. She told me she was going to let you sleep in. I should also let you know why I moved my room to this floor. I want to be close when you need me, just as I was on the third-floor with your grandmother. Never be afraid to ask for help. I'm heading to bed. Sweet dreams, darlin'," she said, as she closed her door.

I stepped into my bedroom and locked my door. Knowing it would be safe to go talk to Greg. I checked my pocket to make sure the mirror was still there, and I peered in the mirror to see how I looked. I quickly put a brush through my hair before standing in front of my full-length mirror. I focused on his truck and went into the mirror. He was not at the truck yet, so I texted him to let him know I was there.

He must have read the text because he came right out. He unlocked the truck and sat in the driver's seat. As I looked at him, I could tell he did not know how to ask me the many questions that were probably floating in his head.

"My family has been protecting the Bloom of Dreams since the late eighteen hundreds. I must protect this stone." I ran my fingers across the stone around my neck. "This stone has certain powers and in the wrong hands could be unbelievably bad. My grandmother was its protector, she passed it on to me. My mother knows nothing about the Bloom of Dreams. I can't stress enough that you must tell no one. I had no choice about exposing it to you because the stone and our lives were in danger."

"I don't understand how it works," he said.

"Honestly, I'm not sure either. This is all new to me, but to use the stone, I must be able to see my reflection. The stone shouldn't be used for evil. I believe the Granaldi family intends to take the stone and use it for their own selfish reasons. The stone warns me when they are near. I must find out why they need it," I said as I continued thinking about the Granaldis. "I need to find out more about them before I head to Italy."

"Italy?" Greg asked.

"Remember, the Granaldi brother's father lives there. He must be the one that wants the stone," I said as I took my mirror from my pocket.

Greg grabbed my hand and said, "I was really worried about you when he grabbed you. I… Well, I kinda like you."

Feeling my cheeks warm, and the butterflies stirring again, "I am very fond of you too," I said with a smile.

"Lisa is right, I need to teach you some martial arts," he said, as he caressed my fingers.

My body tingled at his touch. *Is this happening?* "I would like that. I need to head home. I am tired," I said as I opened my mirror. I turned to him and said, "Goodnight."

I concentrated on my room and just before I left; I heard Greg say goodnight. I nearly hit the bed when I returned. I got up and headed to the bathroom to prepare for bed.

Thirteen

I woke up to the sun shining through my window and remembered it was Sunday. Mom was researching local churches today. I pulled myself out of bed to get dressed. All I wanted was a cup of coffee with my breakfast. The rays streaming through the stain-glass window along the staircase brought a smile to my face. A beautiful day awaited me.

Phyllis sat in the dining room reading the newspaper and drinking hot tea.

"Good morning, Phyllis," I muttered.

She glanced at me with a smile, "There's coffee and coffee cake in the kitchen."

Grabbing my coffee and coffee cake, I again took in the view from the kitchen window. Leaving Phyllis to her paper, I headed outside. I opened the backdoor, grabbed the cake saucer and my coffee. Hands full, I could not shut the door. *You didn't think this through, Brooke.* I put my coffee on the ground and closed the door. I grabbed my coffee and headed to the patio table.

As I placed everything on the glass table, I nearly spilled my coffee from the table being unlevel on the bricks. I could smell cinnamon from the coffee cake, which was a wonderful aroma in the morning. My mom would make cinnamon rolls, or cinnamon toast for breakfast on rare occasions. Her French Toast was my favorite breakfast because she made it with vanilla, cinnamon, and sugar. Mom was not much of a cook, but this she did well.

I leaned back in my chair and sipped my coffee, thinking about everything I needed to do today. First, find anything I could about the Granaldi family and find out if there was a better way to use the mirror. My landings when exiting the mirror were not working. *How can I prevent being thrown on the floor?* I needed to find a solution, or I could not spy on someone.

Suddenly, my phone vibrated. I pulled my phone from my pocket and saw Greg had sent me a text.

GREG: Are you ready for your first lesson? I will be in my garage if you want to join me.

I gulped down the last bit of coffee and placed it on the saucer and headed inside. Phyllis was in the kitchen making herself a to-go cup of tea for church when I entered. Phyllis told me she would take care of my dishes after church and asked me what I had planned for the day.

"Greg is going to teach me karate. I'm headed over there for my first lesson," I informed her.

"That could be a valuable skill for someone like you. Your grandmother was not without some skills herself. Have fun!" she hollered loud enough for me to hear because I quickly left the room. I had not thought about it, but it made sense that my grandmother had to of known how to defend herself. I ran upstairs to brush my teeth and hair. I put my mirror in my pocket before making my way to his garage. As I approached Greg's garage, I found him striking a punching bag with a lot of force. He was only wearing shorts and sneakers. It was very apparent he worked out frequently. He had not noticed me yet, so I took the time to admire his physique. He had a nice tan glistened from the sweat and appeared to have zero fat on his body. His muscles appeared to be etched into his skin. As he punched the bag, a spray of sweat flew off of him. I approached him. He stopped his workout and said good morning to me as he wiped the sweat from his face.

"Good morning," I said, realizing when I saw him how good this day had become. Trying not to be obvious I was admiring him.

"I had a hard time sleeping last night thinking about everything that happened. Knowing what I know now, it is especially important you learn to defend yourself," he said, in an authoritarian voice. "Karate will teach you the skills you will need to deal with armed and unarmed combat."

Greg put two towels on the ground and sat. He motioned for me to sit in the same way as him. He was sitting with his legs crossed and his hands on his knees with his palms up and at an angle toward his face. "First, you need to learn how to meditate to clear your mind. I want you to inhale through your nose and exhale through your mouth. Concentrate on your breathing. Forget the Granaldi brothers, forget your family, forget all your problems. Picture them disappearing before you. Now envision an empty room. He paused for what seemed like several minutes before continuing. Now picture a flame in the center of an empty room. This flame is inner strength and energy. Think about what strengths you wish to gain. Picture those strengths growing and encompassing the room. As your strength grows, the flame grows," he said before remaining quiet for about ten minutes.

I felt so relaxed and inspired to begin my lessons. I concentrated on my room, which was now engulfed in rolling orange and yellow flames, much like a house fire that was overcome by an inferno you would see through one of its windows. Greg moved, so I opened my eyes as he stood. He reached out to help me up, and I waited for my next instruction.

"We are going to warm up." "Follow my lead." We stretched. He put his arms above his head with his right hand holding his left elbow. He leaned to his right side. We did this for another ten seconds before we did the other side. Our second stretch had us standing with our backs next to a wall, and we twisted our torso to the left and turned our head to the right. We did this for another ten seconds and we reversed sides. With each exercise, I found myself counting to see how long we held stretch. We completed several other stretches.

I found myself struggling. *This is harder than I thought, or I'm completely out of shape.* I could feel the burn in my legs from him having me hold the positions. My body was screaming at me, "What are you doing to me?" I was so out of shape. It has been several years since I took a physical fitness class.

When we finished, he told me to follow him, as he headed out of the garage jogging. I thought he was going to teach me karate moves so I could fight like Jackie Chan. I quickly caught up with him. We went a few blocks before it felt like I was dying. I didn't think I had run since my freshman year physical education class. It was when I realized, I was completely embarrassed by how out of shape I had become. The pain in my side was so bad, I was having a hard time breathing.

We were nearly back, and I was ready to stop when Greg turned to me, "I'll race you back." He took off.

Are you kidding me? I tried to run to catch up with him, as my side hurt more. I pushed through the pain and when I caught up with him; he was standing in the garage, barely out of breath. I felt like I was about to collapse. I bent over holding my knees trying to breathe. "Air. I need air."

He looked over at me and smiled, "We've got some work to do to get you in shape." He threw me a clean towel, and I wiped my face as it became easier to breathe.

"We are now going to focus on your stance and balance," he picked the towels off the floor and placed them on a chair in the corner.

Is he trying to tell me we are doing more today? "I thought you were going to teach me kicks, punches, and things," I said confused and thinking, how would my balance save my life.

"To throw strikes or to have powerful kicks, you must have the right stance and outstanding balance," he explained. "First, the front stance, put your feet shoulder-width apart, and bend your right knee and push your left knee back," he said before demonstrating.

I moved into position.

Greg said, "Always bend your knee until you can't see your toes and your back leg must be as straight as you can get it." He looked at my form. "That's it, now try to face your back foot, so it is pointing forward as much as you can."

I held this stance for a minute and felt my muscles burn. I could not control my balance and stance. "These hurt," it amazed me at the trouble I was having with the basics.

He taught me the back stance which would allow me to remain standing if someone swept my front leg and the horse-riding stance where both my feet are parallel, and my legs were slightly bent and about two feet apart before ending my first lesson. We walked into his house and proceeded to the kitchen. Greg grabbed two Gatorade bottles from the refrigerator, before saying, "Let's head out back."

We made our way to the patio. Their wooden patio table sat in the center of the patio. We sat with our backs to the sun. I looked at my room's balcony. *Could he see me gazing down at him?* The balcony obstructed the view unless I sat right next to the edge or stood close to the edge.

"You did pretty well for your first day," he said, as he leaned back in his chair.

I was completely embarrassed because I was so out of shape. Knowing he was being nice, "Thank you."

"What's your plan before school starts in the fall?" he asked.

"Our movers should be here sometime tomorrow. I have unpacking to do. I want to get settled in before my University of Louisville tour. I also promised my mom I would help her find a job.

She is bored. Back home, she was incredibly involved with our church. I'm sure she will become active in a church once she selects one. Pastor Ellis's Church seems cool, but she still wants to see what else is around to make sure she picks the one she is most comfortable with," I took another sip of Gatorade.

"Are you planning on getting a job?" he asked.

"Before my grandmother's death, I would have because my mom could not afford college, but my grandmother set up a trust, which will pay for it. I think my grandmother would have paid for it if she were alive, but my mother never asked her. My mother is a proud woman. She knew my grandmother did not like my dad. She was against them getting married. My grandmother and mother loved each other, but their differences caused them to bump heads a lot. Now I have the funds for college, my mom doesn't want me working. She wants me to focus on school," I said, checking out his physique again.

"I wish I could help with the moving, but I promised my mom I would go with her to my grandparent's house for the day. We're heading over around ten. How about we have another training session in the morning? Is eight good for you?" he asked.

"Sounds good," I dreaded the workout but looking forward to hanging out with him. "Do you work?"

"No, like your mom, my parents want me to concentrate on school. I work on friends' vehicles from time to time for extra cash and Bill pays me when they need help," he informed me.

"It's good you can make money. My mom gave me a weekly allowance for helping around the house and there were a few kids I babysat for in Florida to earn money. Now, I have no income. I don't think my mom is going to pay me now that we have Phyllis. I don't know how much my mom inherited and whether she can even afford Phyllis, but I think my mother will keep her if she can. Phyllis is like family to us," I realize that Phyllis leaving us was a possibility. "Where's your family?"

"Everyone is at church. They usually grab lunch after church before heading home, but today they are taking my dad to the airport. He needs to be there by three for his flight to Atlanta. He travels a lot with his job," he took another gulp of his Gatorade. "I have been thinking about the Granaldi family. If we could spy on them in Italy, we could figure out why they want the necklace."

"I thought of that, but I don't speak Italian. We would never understand them," seeing the disappointment in his eyes. That got me thinking. My grandmother did not speak multiple languages. What would she have done? I needed to talk to Phyllis. I told Greg I needed to clean myself up and speak with my mother about the events of the night before. He walked me to the iron gate before saying goodbye.

Fourteen

I went in and looked for Phyllis. When I could not find her, I peeked out the window. She had not returned from church. After my shower, I peered out the window to see if Mom or Phyllis had come home. Phyllis had returned. I scampered downstairs to get a little more exercise.

"How was your workout?" she asked.

I told her everything Greg had me do and how out of shape I was. She explained my grandmother took several self-defense classes from someone in Japan. She thought she had learned Kung Fu.

I needed to know more about the Granaldi brothers. I asked if she could provide me additional information about them.

Phyllis explained, "There are rumors about a ring, which is also called the Bloom's Cradle. It is believed when the stone is in the cradle it is even more powerful. No one knows if the story is true or what powers the cradle will possess. The Granaldi family is evil and extremely dangerous. There's one Granaldi that has made it his mission to keep his family from getting the stone. We don't know why, and we don't know his name. Lillie had an encounter with him once. This man helped her get away from his relatives. One can assume he knows what powers the stone possesses and for whatever reason, he does not want them to get it."

"I was considering going to Italy to spy on the Granaldis, but I don't speak Italian. Did Grandma speak Italian?" I asked.

"When wearing the stone, whatever the language, you will hear it in English." She started making sandwiches for us.

I realized I was being rude drilling her with my many questions, so I asked, "How was church?"

Phyllis opened a can of tuna, "It was good. Pastor Ellis told me to tell you hello."

"That was nice of him. Do you mind if I help you prepare lunch?"

"There are some pretzels in the pantry. Grab those unless there is something else you would like to have with your tuna sandwich," she instructed.

I got the pretzels and filled two glasses with ice. "Sweet tea?"

"That sounds nice. How about eating out back?" she asked.

"That sounds perfect."

She grabbed a tray and put the drinks on it. I added a pile of pretzels to both plates before closing it and putting it away. Phyllis grabbed the tray of food and headed to the door. I quickly opened the door for her. When she arrived at the table, she took everything off the tray and adjusted the table's umbrella to keep the sun off us. We sat, and we prayed before eating.

We started talking more about my grandmother. Phyllis explained how blessed she was to join her on so many adventures. She warned me I should get a passport because my grandmother and her found themselves separated and she nearly got in a lot of trouble for not having any identification with her. She continued to explain that many places you stay abroad may want to hold on to the passport while you stay with them.

Mom's car came down the driveway. She stepped out of the car and looked wonderful in her white dress and coral sweater with matching coral heels. Her hair pulled back away from her face. She came over and joined us at the table. Phyllis told Mom she would be back with her sandwich and headed into the house.

"How was church?"

"It was nice, but I like Pastor Ellis better," she said. "Phyllis filled me in this morning about you being attacked last night. It surprised me you did not wake me, but Phyllis said you seemed to be okay when you got home, which is why I did not wake you this morning. I'm concerned about you. Was it the Granaldi brothers that attacked you last night?"

I did not know what to say. If I'm honest with her, she might not let me go anywhere. "I don't think so. We didn't get a good look at them," I said, feeling very guilty for lying to her. I knew I was not telling her the truth to keep her and the stone safe. The less she knew, the better. But I admitted Greg had saved me with his karate moves and that he was training me. She seemed pleased to hear it.

"There is something special about that boy," she said as Phyllis placed her sandwich and tea in front of her.

We continued eating our lunch and talking about the movers and Mom wanting help later looking for a job. Phyllis said she would visit her sister after lunch. She put a Mexican casserole in the refrigerator for us to eat for dinner. She left us the cooking directions on the counter. After everyone finished lunch, we brought the dishes to the kitchen. I told Phyllis I would take care of them so she could leave.

Mom said she was heading to her room to change, while I did the dishes. Phyllis grabbed something from the refrigerator to take with her. When I finished wiping the counters down, I wrote a note for Phyllis on the notepad. It read, "Phyllis, you are a blessing to our family. We love you, B." I headed up to the third-floor. I knocked on my mother's door and announced myself.

"Come in," she hollered from her closet.

I entered her room, "We could use our phone for a hot spot and look for jobs now."

"I had forgotten we don't have Wi-Fi yet; we need to sign up tonight, if possible, cause I need to find a job," she said, as she closed her closet door.

I grabbed a notepad and pen from her desk and her computer. "I'll meet you in the sitting room."

I walked down the hall to the third-floor sitting room. I put the computer on the table and set the computer up with my phone as the hot spot. Mom sat next to me, and we made an appointment with the cable company. We also contacted the electric company and water company about what needed to be done to get everything put in my mom's name. After setting up an account on Indeed.com, we started searching for companies in need of an Executive Assistant. We completed the online applications for several positions and uploaded her resume and cover letters. By the time we finished, it was nearly dinner time.

I headed down to the kitchen and read the directions for the casserole, preheated the oven, and pulled the casserole out of the refrigerator. Wanting to do something special for mom, I set the table and placed fresh flowers from the garden in a vase before heading back to the kitchen to put the casserole in the oven.

Mom came downstairs and thanked me for helping her. She looked at the table and turned to me, "Would you like to invite Greg over for dinner? I would like to thank him."

Surprised by her asking, "I will ask him."

I texted Greg to see if he wanted to join us. He quickly texted back.

GREG: What time?

BROOKE: Dinner will be in about forty minutes, but you can come now.

He texted me back saying he was getting into the shower. I headed back to the kitchen to get another place setting. I ran upstairs to clean myself up before he arrived.

About twenty minutes after I received Greg's last text, he arrived at my door. I let him in, and my mother reached out and gave him a big hug as soon as he entered the foyer.

"I can't thank you enough for saving my daughter, she is all I have," her eyes filled with tears.

I was so surprised she could keep her composure when she was talking to me. I think this affected her a lot more than she let on. Greg just smiled at her. It appeared he did not know what to say.

Mom led us to the drawing-room, where she sat in a chair. We sat on the sofa together. I was surprised he sat so close to me. I felt like a little girl with a new toy. "Brooke tells me you are teaching her karate," she stated.

"Yes, she needs to learn to protect herself. Neither of us is working and with school not starting until August, we have plenty of time to train. We'll train again tomorrow morning," he informed her.

"That's great. The movers won't be here until about ten tomorrow morning. I'll need her here when they arrive. I need her to help direct them," she said.

"We'll make sure we're done by then," he assured her.

Greg spent much of the evening telling us about the University of Louisville, his family, and friends. After dinner, he helped me with the dishes and Mom headed upstairs to call Susie.

Greg and I hung out in the kitchen talking about the Granaldi brothers. I did not want to disclose how I thought I could understand other languages, but I needed to test it out before heading to Italy. So, I told him, "I have a theory. My grandmother traveled the world not knowing other languages, and she had no problem understanding anyone. Perhaps the stone somehow lets you understand other languages."

There was a long pause before he responded, "That could be true. How can we test this?" We both took a minute to think about it, and Greg said, "We can go to Italy."

"The only problem is, I need an image of where we're going. I also can't let anyone see me when I arrive," I said, being discouraged.

"I've got it! My friend Helen Ruiz's father works for Bill, and her mother doesn't speak English well. We could somehow hide in the bushes or something and listen to them," Greg said enthusiastically.

"That's a great idea, but I need an image of her home," I said, hoping he had a picture.

He seemed to be in deep thought for a minute before opening his phone. "She's on Snapchat, let me see what I can find," he scrolled through his phone. Looking disappointed, he said, "No luck." He started going through his phone again. "Got it!" He showed me the picture.

I studied the picture of a girl on a front porch in her cap and gown, "This may work."

Just in case mom came down, I wrote her a note telling her I was going to Greg's house for a few minutes. I opened the pantry door, turned on the light, and pulled Greg in. "I'm going to get us there, and I'm hoping we will both be invisible and God willing we will land on our feet, just in case we are not, find somewhere to hide when we arrive," I instructed.

"Invisible?"

"Yes. I'm not sure it will work. Now, don't let go," I instructed as I opened my mirror. Greg grabbed my arm. I focused on the image from the pictures, arriving invisible, and landing standing. It sucked us into the mirror, and we arrived just next to Helen's porch. We quickly moved behind the bushes. Before putting the mirror back in my pocket, I opened it to confirm I did not see our reflections. I showed Greg the mirror to show him he too was invisible. It was strange, we could see each other, but we were invisible to the world.

Greg whispered, "Follow me."

I started following him around to the back of the house. It did not appear anyone was there. We continued to a window on the back side of the home. Greg looked in. I was not tall enough to see anything. He tapped on the window. It sounded like someone was home, but I could not make out anything they were saying or even what language they were speaking. A woman opened the backdoor and looked out. She turned around as if she searched for someone. Just as she was about to close the door, she said, "Juan."

A young boy appeared, and she said, "See, there is nothing out here. Now, go get in the tub." She shut the door.

Greg whispered, "Did you understand her?"

"Yes," I said.

"Good, the only thing I understood was Juan. That is Helen's little brother. I heard her speaking Spanish," he said.

"I cannot believe it worked. Hang on, we need to get back," I opened my mirror and pictured us standing in the pantry.

When we arrived, Greg said, "I don't know if I'll ever get used to that."

"I know what you mean. Well, we know it works," I said.

"Does this mean we are going to Italy?" he asked, making it very apparent he wanted to join me.

"Yes, but not right away," I opened the pantry door and turned off the light. I grabbed the note I wrote and put it in the trash. As I looked at him, I could see he looked disappointed. "This will be extremely dangerous. I need to be prepared. We need to keep training and when I'm ready, we'll go."

"You're right," he said.

"Look, it's getting late. I need to get up early for my trainer," I said in a flirtatious way.

He delicately squeezed my hand and smiled, "Good night." He gently pulled his hand away and headed to the backdoor.

I smiled back as he walked out the door, "Good night." I headed up to my room to get some rest for the long day tomorrow.

Fifteen

My alarm went off at seven. The excitement of the day got me out of bed quickly. Every muscle hurt. I dressed, making sure I wore comfortable clothes, and headed downstairs. My muscles screamed at me with each passing stair. All I wanted was a cup of yogurt for breakfast. When I arrived at the kitchen, it did not appear Phyllis was up yet. After some searching, I found everything I needed to make a pot of coffee and put the kettle on for Phyllis's hot tea. I looked out the window to make sure she was home. I did not remember seeing her car when Greg left. It was there. Wanting to show her gratitude, I wanted to surprise her with a fried egg sandwich. Grabbing a pan from the cabinet, bacon grease, eggs, and cheese from the refrigerator, I began making egg sandwiches. While I made breakfast, I could feel the pain in my muscles. I tried to stretch out while the eggs cooked.

Phyllis walked into the kitchen, "Good morning. You're up early." She grabbed her apron. "Something smells good."

"Have a seat," I said, proudly. The kettle started whistling, so I turned the burner off.

I placed Phyllis's breakfast and hot tea in front of her and I sat next to her with mine. She thanked me for the meal. We talked about how I was feeling about Greg. She and my mother both think he is pretty amazing. She offered to clean the dishes and would make a sandwich for Mom when she came down. I headed upstairs to brush my teeth and to grab two towels. It was quarter to eight, and I waited for Greg at his garage door.

I did not want to knock on the door because I arrived early. Trying to remember all the stretches, I began stretching my stiff muscles on his driveway. I was sitting on my towel doing my third stretch when the garage door opened. I felt like a deer caught in the headlights.

Greg strolled over, "Look at you." It sounded like it surprised him to see me already stretching. He put his towel down and joined me. Once we finished stretching, we went for a run, going a little farther than the day before. He continued teaching me the basic skills. I listened carefully to his instructions, determined to learn as much as possible from him as quickly as I could. I needed to know how to defend myself if I am going to continue to be attacked.

During training, the moving truck showed up early and I said goodbye. It was a long day, but the movers finally finished and headed out. Mom, Phyllis, and I agreed the day exhausted us. We ordered Chinese and turned in early.

Over the next few weeks, Greg and I trained every day. Each day we reviewed what I had previously learned before he taught me something new. To strengthen my skills more, I did extra training when he was not around. I have a feeling; I was making Phyllis and Mom crazy running up and down the stairs trying to get into shape. There had been no sign of the Granaldi brothers since we saw them at Austin's farm.

I was still not ready to go to Italy. In those few weeks, I had learned a lot and was in the best shape of my life.

The day came to head to the University of Louisville for my tour. Mom gave me her car because she had begun using my grandma's Cadillac. Her new job, which will start next week, would require her to travel a lot with her boss. As much as I would miss Mom being around, it meant not needing to be so careful when transporting and spying.

I was up at six for a quick workout by myself. The workouts were becoming enjoyable. After showering, I put my hair in a loose braid that came down over my left shoulder. *Hum, what should I wear for a tour with Greg?* Finally selecting jeans, a navy-blue V-neck t-shirt, and my crossbody purse. I did not want to carry anything. Making sure I put my mirror in my purse. It was nearly nine. Greg will be here soon. I took my time heading down the stairs to prevent myself from sweating. I heard Phyllis and my mother's voices as I made my way to the first floor. Following the sound, I found them chatting in the dining room. We chatted for a few minutes about mom's new job. We heard the doorbell. My heart started racing. It brought me so much joy being with Greg.

I greeted Greg and followed him to his truck. He opened the passenger door and patiently waited for me to get settled into my seat before shutting the door. I was so excited about heading to college. We arrived early at the campus because Greg wanted to take pictures of me at the University of Louisville sign. Tammy, our tour guide, seemed to know everything about the University. Greg showed me where some of his classes were the previous semester. He also ran into a few friends. The campus was beautiful and everyone we met was so nice, but its size was a little overwhelming.

We grabbed a bite to eat at the Old Louisville Tavern. I ordered the Spicy Chipotle Burger and Greg got the BBQ Bacon Burger. It was so delicious. When we got done eating, we sat around talking about the University and flirted a bit.

Greg had been looking around the restaurant. Unexpectedly, he moved his chair closer to mine. He wrapped his arm around the back of my chair and leaned in closer to me. My heart started racing. *Is he about to kiss me? Oh no, I just ate onions!*

He grabbed my hand, "Don't turn around."

I looked him in the eyes. I could tell the Granaldis are back.

I acted like I was flirting with him, I leaned toward him, "They're here, aren't they? What's the plan?"

"He's at the front door. We could exit through the back of the restaurant, "he suggested as he adjusted his seat. He leaned his body toward me and smiles, "The ladies room is in the back of the restaurant," he pulled thirty dollars from his wallet and placed it on the table. "Get up. Act like you are going to the bathroom. When you reach the ladies room door, make a break for the exit door. I will start running as soon as you do." Greg moved his chair back, "Okay he is sitting down now. Go ahead but stay calm."

I got up and headed toward the backdoor. When I was about halfway there, I turned around in a flirtatious way and blew Greg a kiss, while I glimpsed at Joseph. I turned back toward the exit. As I got to the ladies room, I took a deep breath and bolted to the backdoor. Nearly running over a server coming out of the kitchen. As I went to push the back door open, I realized Greg had already caught up with me. We ran out the door to find Tony waiting for us. Greg shoved me out of the way and used the backhand strike. He turned toward him with a knee kick, followed by a rising punch. Tony tried to block him but was unsuccessful. We made a break for the building to the east of the restaurant. With a quick turn between the first two buildings, we slid behind a row of bushes. There were windows everywhere. It was not safe to teleport out of the area.

Tony drove slowly down West Gaulbert Avenue while Joseph walked on the other side of the buildings. We need to make our way back to Greg's truck.

Greg said, "It is not safe here. I will distract them." He tossed me the keys to his truck. "There is an elementary school just down the road. I will head them east toward the school. I want you to go to the intersection of West Lee Street and South 5th Street. If I am not there in 20 minutes' head home. I will get an Uber and call you." His eye surveyed the area before taking off toward the school. I watched Joseph to make sure he noticed him. He must of because he put his phone in his pocket and started running.

When I knew the coast was clear, I ran back to the restaurant and locked myself in Greg's truck. I was out of breath. I pulled out my phone to find the intersection I needed to be at. My hands shook, making it hard to find the location. These men were dangerous and now Greg was dealing with them alone. I took a deep breath to calm my nerves.

As soon as I found the intersection, I started the truck and headed to the location. I arrived there but did not see Greg anywhere. *Lord, please let him be okay.* I was watching my watch to make sure that twenty minutes had not passed. My mind was racing thinking about the many things preventing Greg from making it here. *Please be okay.* It had only been fifteen minutes. I did not have anywhere to park, so I went around the block and made my way back to the intersection. It was now past the twenty minutes. I was hoping he did not think I left him. I turned left onto South 5th Street. I saw Joseph looking defeated. Greg must have gotten away. I slowly went down the road, not knowing where to look for Greg, when he flew out from behind a car, and I nearly ran into him. I unlocked the door and let him in.

"We need to get out of here," he said, as he looked behind him.

We both agreed we lost them. Greg let me drive his truck back home.

"Remember, we can't tell anyone about this," I reminded him. My emotions got the best of me. I felt tears in my eyes.

"I know. I'm so glad you are okay," he reached over to touch my hand.

"Me? I was worried about you," I said shocked by his comment. We spent the rest of the ride home on high alert and talking about the chase and our tour. I parked in his driveway and gave him his keys. "Come on, let's tell my mom about the college."

We told Mom and Phyllis about the tour, everyone we met, and showed them the pictures we took. "We had lunch at The Old Louisville Tavern," I informed her. Greg shot me a look that said, "What are you doing?" I think he was afraid I would mention the Granaldi brothers. "We both had burgers there, and they were delicious. We need to go there some time, Mom."

It was still early, so Greg suggested we train. I already practiced a few moves that morning, but after that day I think I needed to train as often as I could. After changing, we met in his garage. Our training became more intense. I have received over twenty hours of training so far. I knew the jab-cross, up block, snap kick, down block, and front kick. We worked on ridge hand, hammer fist, and the back-sidekick. Greg told me I impressed him with how quickly I was progressing.

After our workout, I headed home to shower. When I walked in, my mother was in the sitting-room on the phone. "I am looking forward to it. I know Brooke will be excited to meet you too." Without looking up, she held up her finger. Which meant I needed to stay because she would be off the phone in a minute.

Mom hung up, "I have a surprise for you, I just got off the phone with my cousin, Phillip. He is coming here for a visit this weekend. I have not seen Phillip since I was about twelve."

"That is exciting," I said, realizing most of our relatives I had met had passed on. "When will he be here?" I asked.

"He is flying in Friday night from New York," she answered. She stood, "He will stay in the second-floor guestroom. I need to tell Phyllis," she said with excitement as she headed to the kitchen.

I rushed to my room to clean up for dinner, distracted by the thoughts of the Granaldi brothers. They will do anything to get the Bloom of Dreams. I believed they have the ring, but what occupied my thoughts was, how was it connected to the stone. *There must be something on the internet.* I opened my computer and researched the Granaldi family and the ring. I found nothing.

I tried to find more information about Anthony Granaldi III. Still nothing. *Think, Brooke.* I remembered what Phyllis mentioned: the Granaldi family wanted the stone, and they may have been looking for it before my family acquired it. I immediately started researching older members of the Granaldi family. There was nothing on Anthony Granaldi II.

Anthony Granaldi was another story. I found a black-and-white picture of him from 1854. The photograph was of him and his wife, Maria. She was sitting next to him. Maria had dark curly hair that was pulled up in the back. The placement of her hands did not allow me to see if she was wearing rings. A beautiful necklace adorned her neck, but it was not the Bloom of Dreams. I turned my attention to Anthony; he had on a nice suit, which included a vest and a tie around his neck that resembled the type of tie Colonel Sanders would wear. I was just about to close the tab when I realized Anthony was wearing a ring.

I zoomed in on the picture, but I could not blow the picture up enough to get a clear picture of the ring. Leaves were going up the side. I continued my search to see if I could find a better picture of the ring. After searching through many rings of that era, I finally found a ring that looked similar. I pulled both pictures up to compare the images. Both rings had the same pattern on the side of the ring. *Found it!* It looked as though there were leaves that grew up the edges of the ring and made a "V". In the open area of the "V" was the same Bloom that was on the Bloom of Dreams, and it looked as if the Bloom of Dreams was in the ring. I saved a copy of the ring and took a picture to show Greg later.

Sixteen

During dinner, Mom told us about what she remembered about Phillip. It was not much. Her mother did not seem to be very fond of his father. Mom attributed her mother's dislike of his dad to the reason she and Phillip saw little of each other when they were children. She remembered Phillip being a little younger than her. As my mom and Phyllis continued their conversation about what to make for meals during his stay, my mind was scrolling through everything Greg has taught me so far. I've still got so much to learn, but I had come a long way. It is hard to remember how out of shape I was. I'm in the best shape I have ever been in. When I moved here, I could barely run around the block. Now I can easily run a couple of miles. Phyllis got up and started clearing the table. Mom and I helped her clean up before we all retired to our rooms for the night.

Over the next few days, I focused on my training. I needed to be ready for Italy because I did not know what we would be up against, and we needed to defend ourselves.

Friday morning started like any other day. I got up and was getting ready to train. Greg texted, he could not meet me, but he would leave the garage door open so I could use the punching bag. He had to pick his dad up from the airport.

I did my stretches before heading out for my run. As I ran, I focused on my breathing. Many people were out enjoying the day. Occasionally passing another pedestrian or runner. Greg and I made sure we covered no less than two miles, which meant hitting several blocks twice. I had finished my first mile; when I sensed someone was watching me. Scanning the area to see if my gut was right. I saw the usual pedestrians. Paying closer attention to my surroundings, I ran at a slower pace. I turned the corner and jumped behind some bushes on the side of someone's house. Ducking down, I peered through the branches. Almost feeling like I was losing it. A blue Mazda drove by. It did not appear to be acting suspiciously.

About thirty seconds later, a black Toyota Camry stopped at the stop sign. The car was too far away to see the passengers. The vehicle had plenty of openings to move. It just sat at the stop sign even when no other cars were at the four-way stop. Finally, it turned right, heading in the direction I was running. It leisurely made its way down the road and stopped just in front of me. The stone warmed. The passenger's side window went down, and Tony and Joseph were looking straight at me. Joseph jumped out of the car and started heading in my direction.

Bolting out from behind the bush and headed back in the direction I came from with Joseph on my tail. Needing to make it back home, I cut through yards to get back quicker. Turning left into a yard, disappointed to find a tall fence.

I tried to get over the fence. My first attempt was unsuccessful. Backed up for my second attempt. I started running to the fence to make it over. Turning around was not an option. Joseph was right behind me. I had my hands on the top of the fence and was trying to pull myself over it when Joseph grabs my leg. He tried to get me down.

I kicked him in the head before falling off the fence. He started coming after me again. Hitting him with a jab-cross in the face, followed by a snap kick to the chest. I noticed Tony had located us and was still in his car by the road. On the third attempt at the fence, I finally pulled myself over without Joseph catching me.

I ran through the backyard and made my way over the fence to the neighbor's yard behind them. There was a lady weeding. Running through her yard to the next street. I turned right and headed down the street. Crossing over and cutting through another yard. I sprinted and tossed myself over a chain-linked fence to find a German Shepard lying on the owner's patio. We both looked surprised to see each other.

I slowly made my way toward the back of his yard. "Nice doggy." My heart raced even faster. He tilted his head to the left before quickly jumping up and barking at me. I turned toward the fence in the back of his yard, and I raced as fast as I could as he chased after me. I grabbed the fence and swung my legs over it as he jumped up, trying to bite me. He continued barking at me as I ran through the next yard.

I finally reached my street. Tucking myself out of view on the side of a neighbor's home. Peered out searching for the Granaldi's vehicle. I saw them approaching. Making a break toward the backyard but making sure I could still see the road if the car passed by. The hood came into sight. It was moving like molasses down the road as the Granaldis looked for me. I made sure I was out of sight as they passed. From a window, I heard a man holler to get out of his yard. I returned to the spot on the side of the house to watch them inch their way toward my house.

As soon as they passed my house, I made my way toward it, hiding behind bushes and cars to prevent them from seeing me. Only a few more houses to get past before I am home. Starting to feel confident I had lost them. I was about to make a break for my home when, they pulled into a driveway to turn around and head back toward me. I rushed to the back of the closest house and hid in their backyard.

I tried to focus on slowing down my breathing, when a man's voice said, "Can I help you?" I turned to see a man sitting on his patio chair reading a book.

"I am so sorry. I was on my morning run when two guys started following me," I said as I continued to catch my breath. "They are down the road near my house."

"I knew you looked familiar; I've seen you with a young man a few times. Do you want me to call the police?" he asked.

I paused a moment to consider his offer. The less my mom knew about my encounters with the Granaldi brothers, the better. "No, I'm sure when they think I'm gone, they'll move on," I said, wondering if they were still there.

"Stay as long as you like," he said as he returned to his book.

I waited a few more minutes. Wiping the sweat dripping in my eyes, before sneaking back to the side of the house to view the road. Checked both directions. I did not see them anywhere, so I sprinted as fast as I could back to my house. I noticed Greg's garage was still open. Afraid to take a chance to close it, I opened the iron fence and quickly closed it. Searching again for the Camry on my street. There was no sign of them. I went inside and locked the door behind me.

Mom sat at the desk reading mail. "You're back early."

Trying to come up with a reason for cutting my training short, I said, "Greg took his dad to the airport." I thought to myself that was sort of true. I hated lying to her. The rest of the day I helped Phyllis and Mom make sure the house was clean, and we helped Phyllis prep for dinner. Mom asked me to go to the airport with her. Phyllis was staying home to make sure dinner was ready when we arrived. I made sure I was ready before Mom came down. I grabbed the sign my mother had me make with Phillip's name from the desk and waited for her in the drawing-room. Mom came down in a blue dress that complimented her figure perfectly. I told her how beautiful she looked. She complimented me too before we headed out the door.

On the ride to the airport, Mom and I talked about all the changes that have happened since Grandma passed. Mom would start her new job Monday, and I would start school soon after. We decided apart from the loss of my grandmother, things in our lives were looking up. Mom was so excited about her new position.

We parked the car in the short-term parking area and headed to the luggage claim with the sign. We found seats near the luggage carousel because his flight had not arrived. Mom called Susie to see what she has been up to, and I texted Greg about what had happened earlier with the Granaldi brothers and apologized for leaving his garage door open. He did not seem worried about it at all. He leaves it open frequently. He told me his dad was looking forward to meeting me.

The carousel moved. I nudged Mom, pointed to the carousel to let her know he would be here soon. She nodded and continued her conversation until people arrived. Once she hung up the phone, we made our way closer to the carousel but making sure we were not in anyone's way of getting their luggage. I stood, making sure the sign was visible. An attractive man about six feet tall with brown slicked-back hair started heading our way with a suitcase. He looked like he might be about the same age as my mother and was wearing a black fitted collared shirt that complemented his build, black jeans, and black oxfords.

As he approached my mother he said, "Sandra?"

She looked at him and smiled before hugging him. As they ended the hug, Mom told him how she was so glad he came. She turned and introduced me to Phillip. After the introductions, we headed back to the Cadillac. The entire ride home, Phillip and Mom talked about the few times they were together as children. I paid little attention to their conversation. I was texting Greg about the events of the day. Before I knew it, we were in the driveway.

Before entering, I put the sign in the trash. We entered the house through the back door and Phyllis greeted us. My mother asked me to put Phillip's suitcase in his room. I did as she instructed, before returning to join them. Mom and Phillip were sitting at the table waiting for me to start dinner. Phyllis brought salads for each of us and returned to the kitchen. I noticed there was not a place setting for Phyllis. "Mom, why is Phyllis not joining us?"

Phillip's eyebrow went up. He seemed surprised and annoyed I had inquired. Mom looked at the table and must have noticed I was correct, "I am not sure."

In a very arrogant way, Phillip asked, "Your cook eats with you?"

"Yes, she is like family," I snapped.

Mom shot me a look to tell me to watch my mouth. Annoyed at our snobbish guest. My mother glared at me. Smiling, I asked, "What do you do for a living?"

Phillip informed me he was in real estate because it allowed him to travel when he wanted to.

Is he staring at my necklace? Stop being paranoid.

Phyllis brought out the second course, which was short ribs braised in red wine, with mashed potatoes and roasted carrots. The meal was so good, I could not believe I helped her prepare it.

Phillip inquired about Grandma. He seemed extremely interested. Mom began telling him about her world travels, which included trips to Japan and Italy.

I interrupted, "Where in Italy?"

Phillip sat up in his chair with his eyes fixed on my mother. He seemed to be interested in hearing the answer.

My mom thought for a minute, "Florence, I think?"

Phillip added, "Florence, is a beautiful city with many masterpieces of Renaissance architecture. The Duomo is a sight to see. It is a cathedral with a terracotta tile dome. Do you know why Aunt Lillie was there?"

"She loved to travel. I know she loved Italy," Mom said, as Phyllis cleared the plates.

Phillip kept going on about his experiences in Italy until Phyllis brought out the Crème brûlée. As we ate, he turned his attention to me, "Is that the necklace, Aunt Lillie always wore?"

My mother paused before confirming it was. She seemed disappointed she did not get the necklace when she told him I inherited the necklace from Grandma.

He started asking me more about myself, wanting to know about my school, hobbies, and my schedules. His questions seemed intrusive, so I answered them without providing too much information. I do not think my mother liked my less informative answers, because she started telling him about my workout schedule, when school would start, and about my friends.

Not knowing why, I did not like this guy, but the stone did not seem bothered by him. I tried not to let him bother me. I excused myself from the table, taking his plate with mine to the kitchen. Phyllis sat on the stool eating her dinner.

"Phyllis, I'm so sorry, you're not in there," I said as I approached her.

She finished chewing her rib, "It's fine. I didn't join your grandmother for dinner when she had guests."

I put the plates on the counter. Phyllis got up. I told her to sit, and I would clear the table. She should enjoy her meal. I went out and grabbed my mother's plate and silverware, when Phillip said, "Shouldn't your cook be doing that?"

I ignored him and continued clearing the table. I walked back into the kitchen and started rinsing off the plates and putting them in the dishwasher, but he annoyed me. I am sure it must have shown.

Phyllis asked, "Is something bothering you?"

I firmly but quietly said, "I don't like him. He's an obnoxious snob." There was a long pause before I continued, "He's going to be here until Sunday. He's practically a stranger. Mom has not seen him for years and wouldn't have recognized him if he walked up to her on the street. If his dad was anything like him, I understand why Grandma kept her distance. What's Mom thinking letting a stranger in our home?"

"Catch your breath, dear," Phyllis said, as she eased me away from the sink. "Let's not take it out on the dishes."

Phyllis and I finished cleaning the kitchen, while Mom and Phillip went to the drawing-room. Phyllis brought them coffee and returned to the kitchen. I was retreating to my bedroom, I passed in front of the entrance to the drawing-room when Phillip asked, "Brooke, do you mind taking me on a tour of this amazing house tomorrow?"

Excusing myself, I informed him I had some research to do. *I am researching you! I do not trust this guy.* I pulled out my computer and started searching Phillip Davis, New York City. There were thirty-five results. I added real estate to the search, and I found him. It appears he told us the truth about himself. According to the article from NY Success Magazine, he had many properties throughout New York and New Jersey. I found nothing to say he was evil or anything. I put my computer away and listened to music while I played games on my phone.

I did not realize it was getting late until my mom and Phillip started climbing up the stairs. She was showing Phillip to his room. I heard her say good night before I heard footsteps on the stairs. I got up and closed the door before changing for bed myself.

In the middle of the night, the Bloom of Dreams woke me as the stone warmed. I was facing the window with my back to the door. Grabbing my phone to check the time. It was one. The stone was not burning like it got when the Granaldi brothers are nearby. It was trying to tell me something. I laid there still. I heard every creak the house made. When I heard what sounded like my door closing, I flipped over and turned on my light. Nothing was there. I tip-toed to the door. Listening for noise from the other side. I heard nothing, so I opened the door and looked down the hall. There was no one there. I closed the door and locked it. Something told me to get my mirror, I went to my purse, and it was open, which was odd because I always closed it. My mirror was not there. I panicked. *Did someone come into my room and take the mirror?* I reached up and checked my neck to see if my necklace was still there. Relieved when I felt it. I started thinking about the last time I saw my mirror, and that is when I remembered I never took it out of my pocket after my run. Digging in my hamper to grab my shorts. I squeezed the pocket and felt relieved when I discovered the mirror was still there.

I had a hard time going back to sleep. *Had Phillip been in my room?* There was no way I was going to let him get the stone or the mirror. I needed to keep a close eye on him.

Seventeen

The next morning, I got ready for my workout. I put the mirror in my bra so Phillip could not find it. I headed to the kitchen. Phillip caught my eye as I passed the drawing-room, I noticed Phillip was looking for something. He moved his search area to the bar. *What is he looking for?* "Do you need something?"

Phillip's body jerked at my voice as he turned around. "No, I'm just admiring the antiques in the home. Your grandmother had superb taste."

Not believing him, I headed to the kitchen to grab a yogurt and coffee for breakfast. Phyllis was washing strawberries. I told Phyllis about his suspicious behavior and of suspecting him of being in my room. She advised me to spy on him before my mom came down. She was right. I went into the pantry, turning on the light before grabbing the mirror from my bra. I concentrated on being invisible in the foyer. Arriving in the foyer; I glanced at the mirror to ensure I was invisible before sneaking to the doorway of the drawing-room. He was opening drawers looking for something, not admiring the antiques. *What could he be looking for?* He must be looking for the mirror. He knew I had the stone. Mom came down the stairs. I looked at the mirror and concentrated on the pantry. Quickly exiting the pantry, I told Phyllis he was looking for something. Mom walked in and asked if breakfast was ready. I sat on the stool at the kitchen counter to eat my yogurt and drink my coffee. The last thing I wanted was to be near him. I headed to Greg's house early.

Greg was opening the garage when I arrived. I filled him in on everything going on with Phillip. He laid his towel on the ground. That is when I realized I forgot my towels. Greg told me to take his. He headed back into the house and returned with another towel. I had already begun stretching when he returned with a man the same height as him. I rose to greet the man.

"Brooke, this is my dad, Andrew," Greg said, as his dad held out his hand to shake mine.

I said, "It's nice to meet you."

"Dad's going to join us for today. I've been telling him how well you are progressing. He wants to spar with you," Greg said as Andrew laid their towels on the garage floor.

"Don't worry Brooke, I'm out of shape and not nearly as good as Greg," Andrew reassures me.

Once we finished stretching, we went for a run, but we did not run our normal two miles. I think Greg was being nice to his dad because he seemed to struggle a bit. As we ran, I looked for the Granaldi brothers, but I did not see them. When we returned to the garage, each of us took turns practicing our punches and kicks on the punching bag. After we warmed up, Andrew and I put on our pads to prepare for our sparing match, while Greg put mats down on the ground. We both put our helmets on and bowed to one another.

I made sure I was concentrating on my balance as I hit him with a snap kick, which is when you lift the knee and snap the lower leg into the target. Andrew blocked it. I lifted my knee and moved my lower leg straight forward, performing a front kick followed by a jab-cross. I landed the jab-cross, but he blocked my kick. Andrew retaliated with a round kick by lifting his knee while turning the foot he was standing on and his body in a semicircular motion and extending his leg with the lower part of his shin, but I could dodge it. We continued sparing with each of us getting a few hits in, but I think I hit him more than he could get me because he was getting worn out.

My last kick hit him hard in the chest. I think I kicked him too hard because he said, "Okay, I've had enough." He backed away from me and tried to catch his breath.

Greg helped me get the pads off and helped his father.

"I am so sorry," I said to Andrew.

"What are you sorry for? You did a fantastic job. You are an impressive young lady," he sat down on a chair in the garage's corner and wiped the sweat from his forehead.

Greg reassured, "Wow, you have come farther along than I thought."

I felt proud. I was careful not to seem too prideful.

"Oh, we're not done yet. Grab your towel and water bottle. We are going for a ride," Greg instructed.

Andrew told us to have fun and headed into the house. After about twenty minutes, we pulled into a warehouse area and parked. I grabbed my things and followed Greg toward the building. As he was about to open the glass door to the building, I read the sign on the door, Parkour 4U. *We are doing a parkour course.*

He smiled and held the door as I entered. They covered the floor with pads and there were a lot of different size and shaped structures that were different heights throughout the room. There were platforms, bars, foam pits. There was also a strength training area. "This place looks incredible," I said.

Greg paid for us to get in and we signed a waiver before entering. Placing our things in a locker before he turned to me, "I want you to follow me and try to keep up. We're going to start in the beginner area. We will progress to another level if I have confidence in your skills."

We stretched before heading to the first beginner's area. There were four bars about seven feet tall. I stood there watching people pulling themselves up, so their chests were above the bar before they did a backflip off the pole. Another guy jumped up to the rod and swung his knees over the one in front of him. He let his body swing past the bar until the back of his knees were secure on to the next one and he grabbed it. Greg pointed to the man, "That's what I want you to do. Ready?"

I tried to jump up to reach the bar but being 5'4" had its disadvantages. After several failed attempts, I felt like everyone was staring and waiting on me. Greg lifted me. I swung my body and could get the back of my leg to the next bar. Greg started encouraging me as I mentally prepared myself to let go. Once released, I swung my body and grabbed the next bar. Tightly gripping the bar before releasing my legs from the other pole. I swung myself to the mat just outside of the structure. Stuck the landing, even though I wobbled for a second, I did not fall or move my feet. I insisted on trying it again. I did better the second time, but still moving like a turtle through the structure.

We moved on to some colored boxes that were a variety of shapes, sizes, and colors. The first box was blue. We ran up it, before jumping to a green box that appeared to be a little higher and was about four feet away. The next box was yellow. It was about three feet lower than the green box. Greg asked me to watch him as he did the course. As he ran up the ramp, I noticed they were hard foam. That comforted me. Greg did the course like a pro. I approached the blue ramp. *You've got this.* I took a deep breath before I ran toward the green box; I did not hesitate as I leaped and made it across to the box. My left foot was partially off the block that was only a foot wide. I focused on my balance. Reaching the yellow box felt like an accomplishment. I jumped down to the floor.

People across the room were doing flips over a small structure and landing on a beam on the floor. I hoped Greg did not think I was going to try that. We headed over to an area with a mat that went up the wall. Two feet above the mat was a bar. I watched the people running up the mat, a few grabbed the bar, and a few did not and fell. Unsure of myself, I insisted Greg go first; I watched him run full force toward the wall, and he ran up it like it was nothing. He grabbed the bar, and he turned around and kind of slid down the mat. I could make it part of the way up the wall, but not even close to grabbing the bar.

We went to another area with two walls that were parallel to one another, and one wall was lower than the other wall. Greg went first again to show me what to do. He ran up the tall wall and pushed himself off the taller wall, twisting his body to permit him to grab the top of the shorter wall before repeating the process back to the taller wall. He went through the hole in that wall and jumped on a low beam before returning to me. "You're up."

I tried to attempt the actions he did and made it to the second wall but found myself sliding down.

Greg came over, "Do you know what you did wrong?"

"I didn't go high enough on the first wall." *You can do this*. I took a deep breath in and as I exhaled, I sprinted for the taller wall. Success, I made it to the second wall. I looked behind me to see where I needed to go before attempting the taller wall. Leaping for it, I missed. My body slammed into the wall, and I slid back down to the bottom. My confidence slid away. I was feeling defeated, but I was not giving up.

"Don't hesitate." Greg advised.

On my third attempt, I did not hesitate and made it through the hole in the taller wall, but I missed the landing on the beam and fell on my butt. I continued a few more times before I could land on the beam. We tried a few more things before I realized we had not been in the beginner's section. We worked on the course alone. I went back to the areas I enjoyed. We met at the front when we had enough. I finished first. I felt exhausted.

Eighteen

We started heading back to the house and discussed Phillip's strange behavior. Greg suggested I spy on him some more. I told him I planned on it. He told me he meant now and explained to me that no one would notice me leave the car.

He was right, why not right now? I pulled my mirror from my bra and wiped the sweat off it on my towel. I opened the mirror and pictured myself in the foyer and invisible. Mom sat at the dining room table on a call. Phillip was nowhere in sight. I quietly made my way up to the second floor. I heard someone in the library, but they shut the door. I opened the mirror and pictured myself invisible in the library by the window. Upon arriving, I found Phillip moving books and items on the shelf. He moved to the desk, which was next to me. Phillip was rummaging through the desk, he seemed to smell the air and looked in my direction. He smelled again, before saying, "Brooke?"

Shocked, I held my breath. *Did he smell me?* I lifted my arm a little and smelled my armpit. *Yikes!* It was no wonder he suspected me being there. I needed to get out of here. I opened my mirror and went back to Greg's truck, landing on the seat. My reappearance startled Greg.

"He knew!" I went to lock my seatbelt. "I found him in the library looking around and as he got near me, he could smell me. He called out my name. What do I do now?" I felt short of breath.

"He didn't see you. He suspected you were there, but he doesn't know for sure. We need to change your smell. We'll get lunch and figure out what to do," Greg said as he turned into a pizza parlor.

We got a few slices of pizza and talked about our options. We decided I would take a shower at his house and borrow clothes from his sister before I went home. I needed to get close enough for him to smell me. As soon as we arrived at his house, Karen gave me clothes and I headed to the bathroom to get rid of my stank.

I was glad that I did not run into his family while I was there. Once I dressed, I headed home. When I walked in, Mom was sitting in the drawing-room. Phillip was not around. She told me he was in his room on a call. I made my way to the second floor, making sure he would hear me coming.

He stepped out of the library, "This is quite a collection of books you have here. Is there one that you can recommend?" He stepped into my personal space and inhaled.

He is trying to smell me. "My grandmother loved books. She enjoyed going to old bookstores and finding what she called works of art. I've read several of these books when I was younger. What are you interested in reading about?"

"Not sure. So many of them look interesting. I thought you worked out every morning," he said as he looked at my clothes.

"Not always. I was going to call a friend of mine, but if you want me to help you find something when I'm done, let me know. Did you still want a tour of the house?" I asked.

"Your mother showed me around. I do not have time to read a book in the short time I have here, but if you think of a delightful book, let me know," he said before making his way downstairs.

I called Greg and told him about what had just happened, and I headed downstairs. Mom asked me if I wanted to join her and Phillip on a tour of Louisville. I told her I needed to register for my classes for the fall term.

I sat in the drawing-room and texted my friends in Florida waiting for them to leave. After they left, I went up to the guest bedroom to search through Phillip's things. I opened the door but stood still as I had forgotten how beautiful this room is with its four-poster bed and armoire.

His suitcase was just inside the door next to the night table. It felt empty. I laid it on the bed and searched every pocket but found nothing. The armoire must contain his things. It contained two collared shirts, a black one that may have been the one he was wearing when he arrived. There was another navy-blue collared shirt, a pair of black slacks, a dark blue pair of jeans, and a black blazer. The drawers had underwear and socks. *If I were him, where would I hide something?* I closed the armoire and headed to the bathroom to go through his bathroom bag and found nothing. After inspecting every drawer in the room, under the bed, and in the bathroom, I scanned the room. *What am I missing?* It occurred to me I never checked the pockets of his clothes. I went back to the armoire and went through the jacket. There was something in the inside pocket. I pulled out an old iron key. It looked like it might fit the doors in the house. Phillip must be looking for the lock to this key.

I called Greg for help, "Greg, can you keep an eye out for my mother's car," I explained to him about the key. He agreed to be my lookout.

As I inspected the key, I tried to think about what it might go to. Phillip had been diligently searching the second floor. As far as I knew, he had not been to the third-floor. To save time, I teleported to the third-floor. I tried it on my mom's door, but it did not fit. The third-floor sitting-room door was unsuccessful, and I did not discover another lock. I check Phyllis's old room and still no luck.

There was a narrow door I had never been in at the end of the hall. It was unlocked, but I tried the key in the lock to see if it would work. Again, not the lock I am looking for. I opened the door to find what looked like the attic. It was a large unfinished room with a bunch of stuff in it. I found a lot of old things, chairs, baskets, an old typewriter, boxes, several trunks, a sewing machine, holiday decorations, antique mirrors, etc. I thought to myself, there is no way I could go through these things before they returned. I tried the key in a few of the trunks that I could reach, but no luck. Suddenly my phone rang. I jumped at the sound of it and my heart raced. I answered the phone as I headed back to Phillip's room.

"Your mom is coming down the street," he said.

"Please stall her," I said before hanging up.

The key needed to be returned to his blazer. As I returned the key, I glimpsed of myself in the full-length mirror. Cobwebs and dust-covered me. I put the key back and rushed to my room. I quickly changed clothes and washed the dirt from my hands and face. On the patio, I brushed the cobwebs out of my hair. Greg talked to them in the driveway. I went back and looked in the mirror before heading downstairs. I tried to look casual and started playing on my phone. They entered, Mom said, "Brooke." I pretended not to hear.

As they walked out of the kitchen, she called for me again.

"I am in the drawing-room."

She approached the drawing-room doorway with Phillip and Greg, "Greg is here to see you."

I moved my legs off the couch to make room for everyone. "How did you like Louisville?" I asked Phillip.

Before speaking, he looked me over. I think he noticed I changed clothes. He said, "I have not been here since Sandra and I were kids, so it was nice to see. I had forgotten how big a city it is. We drove by the Belle of Louisville. I rode that steamboat with my father when I was about ten. I told your mother it would be nice to go to Churchill Downs the next time I come down to visit." He went behind the bar and made himself and my mother a drink.

We sat and talked to them for a little while before dinner.

I asked Greg to stay for dinner. Greg and I sat next to each other, and Phillip sat directly in front of me. Phyllis made us a Mandarin Orange Salad, Kentucky Bourbon Marinated Salmon with asparagus and orzo. For dessert, we had a Lemon Meringue Pie. During the meal, Phillip continued to ask me a lot of questions about what I had done for the day.

Mom excused herself and I grabbed Phillips and mom's plate, when Phillip grabbed my arm, "You really should let Phyllis take care of this. It is her job. You are one of the ladies of the house and need to act like it."

Greg looked like he was in as much shock as I was at his comment. I twisted my wrist to release his hold and continued to clear the table. Greg grabbed the glasses and followed me into the kitchen.

When we got in the kitchen, I whispered, "Can you believe that guy? I can't believe he thinks he's coming back here. I can't wait to talk to Mom after he leaves."

We heard Mom ask him where we were. Greg and I went over to eavesdrop on their conversation. We stayed along the wall behind the door.

"Sandra, you now have inherited your mother's estate. You and Brooke need to act like the ladies of the house. Let your cook do her job. If you would like me to come back and help you get your house in order, I will," he scolded her as though he was her parent.

"Phyllis is like family. She has been working here for the last thirty years," Mom informed him.

"Then perhaps it's time to let her go. She is up in age and will likely retire soon if she is not considering it already," he concluded before a chair moved.

Greg and I snuck back into the kitchen. We said nothing until we knew they were not heading our way. I turned to Phyllis, "We need to encourage Mom not to have him back. He's walking all over her. Phillip told her we should get rid of you. He wants us to act more like the ladies of the house," I said sarcastically, while I pretended to be a snobbish sophisticated lady.

Phyllis said, "It sounds like he is a lot like his father. Lillie didn't like his father at all. I doubt your mother will listen to his advice. I don't think you need to worry about it. Now, go do something fun. I will take care of cleaning up."

Greg and I headed to the backyard for some privacy. We sat at the patio table and discussed the key. I told him it was in Phillip's blazer, and we needed to get the key before he left the following day. We decided I needed to get it after he packed. He will make sure it is packed before he leaves. We might ask Mom or Phyllis to distract him. Phyllis would help, but we needed a problem or something that would require both Mom and Phillip's attention.

We returned to find out when he would be leaving. We found them in the drawing-room and joined them. Phillip was sitting in a chair and Mom was on the couch. We sat next to Mom and listened for a while to their conversations about our family.

I found an opening in the conversation, "What time is your flight tomorrow?"

Mom turned to me, "The flight leaves at 11:45 am. We need to leave here by 10:30 am for him to make his flight."

It hit me how I could make sure they are both occupied. "Perhaps Phyllis could make brunch for you tomorrow before he leaves. He won't be so hungry when he arrives in New York. Phillip could pack before brunch and Phyllis could serve brunch by ten."

"That is a great idea. What do you think, Phillip?" she asked.

"That is fine," he said.

"I will tell Phyllis the plan," I said before I rose and headed to the kitchen.

I informed Phyllis she needed to keep them in the dining room from 10:20 am, so we could try to find the key. Our hope, he thinks he lost it. She was to tell us when his bag was ready to be brought downstairs.

Phyllis headed to the drawing-room, and we snuck into the hall to eavesdrop. "Would either of you like coffee?" she asked.

My mother told her she would, but Phillip said nothing. Phyllis returned to the kitchen for the coffee. We returned to our eavesdropping spot as Phyllis walked into the drawing-room. It sounded like she put the coffee on the table.

Phyllis said, "Sir, please let me know when your bag is ready in the morning, so I can bring it to the car for you."

Phillip said nothing.

Phyllis was already down the hall when Phillip said, "Now that is how your staff should behave."

He made my blood boil. We headed back to the kitchen with Phyllis. Greg told me I should just leave like I was going to work out in the morning. I could use the mirror to sneak back into the house when Phyllis texted us that his bag was ready.

We hung out in the kitchen chatting with Phyllis for a while before Greg left. I said goodnight to Phillip and Mom before heading to my room. I wanted to catch up with my friends in Florida before going to bed.

Nineteen

The next morning, I went about my normal routine. I grabbed a yogurt cup and headed to Greg's house. We did not work out because my mind was focused on getting the key. We would make sure they saw us working out when they left. The clock felt frozen. I had arrived at Greg's house at eight and it was only a quarter to nine. Surely, the bag would be ready soon. We continued to wait around, watching the clock, and trying to discuss what the key might open up.

At 9:46 am she texted it is okay for me to go to his bedroom. I opened my mirror and made sure I appeared invisible in his room. His suitcase was open on the bed. *Seriously, he can't even zip his suitcase.* I went through the bag, making sure I did not disturb the way he had everything packed. No sign of the key or the blazer. I zipped the bag up for Phyllis as I heard her coming down the hall.

I whispered, "Phyllis, the jacket is not here."

She grabbed the suitcase off the bed," There was a jacket on the chair by the piano." I followed her down the stairs, making sure it did not sound like two pairs of steps. I saw the jacket on the chair in front of the piano. While Phyllis informed them, she would be right out with their meal, I lifted the jacket to find the key. I pulled it out of the pocket and nearly dropped it on the floor but caught it just before it hit. I opened the mirror and went back to Greg.

As soon as I arrived, I put the key under my towel. While we stretched, I filled him in on what happened. We ran in place for a few minutes to warm up. It was 10:30 am. They were about to leave. I started punching and kicking the bag to make sure I had a decent sweat when they left. It was 10:45 am when they started pulling down the driveway. Mom called me over to her car, so I stopped my workout and Greg started punching the bag while I went to see what she wanted.

"Phillip seems to be missing a key. We tried to find it before we had to leave, but we still cannot find it. Do you know anything about it?" she asked, while Phillip was staring me down.

"No. I'll keep an eye out for it. Is it a house key?" I asked to see if he would be honest.

Mom and I turned to Phillip to see his response, "It was my father's key. He always carried it with him, and since his passing, I carry it with me to remember him. It is a black iron key."

"I'll keep an eye out for it," I headed back to Greg's garage. We continued our workout and discussing what to do next. We decided we would go through the attic in the morning when Mom was at work. That would give us the entire day to see if we could find what the key went to. It was a little hot for a run, so we finished our workout in the air conditioning at Parkour 4U.

Greg had to help his dad with a project when we got back. I headed home to shower, and helped Mom pick out a few outfits for her first week of work. We hung out in her room chatting and I took that time to tell her how I felt about Phillip.

"Please tell me Phillip is not coming back here," I said.

"Why would you say that?" she asked.

"Mom, he's a bully and a snob and he kept talking down to you and telling me what I should and shouldn't do," I told her.

"I think you are being a little hard on him. He is just trying to help us. You just need to spend more time with him," she said.

Did she just say what I thought she said? Spend more time with him. I could see that there was no changing her mind. We finished in her room and I headed to bed because I would have a lot to do the following day.

The next day Greg came over as soon as Mom left for the day. Phyllis said she would let us know when lunch was ready. We made our way to the attic. Greg and I started moving things around to see if we could find anything with a keyhole. We found several trunks, but the key did not work in any of them. After searching for hours, Phyllis called us to lunch. We washed up before making our way to the dining room.

Phyllis served Asian Salad. We told her about our many finds in the attic but still found nothing the key went to.

We headed back up to continue our search. It was nearly 4:00 pm when we finished going through everything and we still had not found what we were looking for. We found great outfits for costumes, though.

Greg headed home, and I took a shower before heading downstairs to help Phyllis with dinner. We were making chicken with olives and artichokes with roasted Brussels sprouts. Dinner was nearly ready when Mom got home. She came in and sat at the counter, impressed I was helping with dinner.

Mom started telling us about her day. "I spent most of the day with the office manager getting all my paperwork completed and finding out where everything is in the office. My office is next to the CEO's office. I have a black desk and two chairs with a view of the Ohio River." She told us she would travel a lot and wanted to make sure I was okay with it.

I assured her I would be fine here with Phyllis, and I had Greg to protect me. Mom and I headed to bed early.

I was up early with Mom before she left for work. She asked, "Phyllis has not found the key. Have you seen Phillip's key?"

"No, but I honestly have not looked. I'll try to see if I can find it today," I assured her. I needed to find the lock to the key, and soon. While I ate my breakfast, I started thinking about the time Phillip was in the library. I texted Greg and explained why I would not be working out. I told him I would be in the library if he wanted to join me.

As soon as Mom left, I rushed to the library and decided I was going to go over every inch of it. I started with the books. I completed searching a few shelves when Greg arrived. He started at the other end of the room, and we went through every book, every vase, and piece of art in the room and still found nothing. We even tugged on the bookshelves to see if they hid a secret compartment. I went to the desk and started ruffling through it. I checked every drawer. I looked under it and still nothing. Greg lifted the rug in the room and found nothing.

What are we missing? I sat there staring at the desk. *National Treasure!*

"Greg, do you remember the National Treasure movie? The Resolute Desk had a secret compartment. Perhaps this one does too," I said as I inspect the desk.

"Maybe," he continued to look at the bookshelves.

I crawled under the desk and pushed and pulled on it. I took the drawers out and still saw nothing. When I went to put the last drawer back into place, I heard something. I put the drawer down and started pushing and pulling on things. Down the edges of the desk was decorative trim. When I pulled on it, I pulled out a small box that had the trim along the edge. I put it on top of the desk and called Greg over. We found a keyhole on the backside. I grabbed the key from my pocket and tried it in the lock. My heart was pounding. Had we just found what Phillip was looking for? The key fit in the lock. Before opening it, I called Phyllis and asked her to come to the library. She needed to be here to see what was inside.

As I waited for Phyllis, I thought about what could be in this small box. I gently shook the box, and it sounded like there was something metal or wooden sliding around. Maybe there was a letter in there, or perhaps another piece of jewelry, or a stone that did something else.

How did Phillip know about whatever this is? How did he know it would be here?

Phyllis arrived and seemed surprised by the secret compartment. I turned the key, and the compartment opened, which revealed another iron key and a piece of paper. The paper did not appear that old. It read Villa Dianella, Florence and there was a number 17 23 13 20 18.

I kept looking back and forth between the key and the piece of paper. "I am guessing we need to go to Italy," I said to Greg.

I decided to wait on putting the desk back together, "Phillip doesn't know we found this. I'll make sure he gets his key back, but we must throw him off the track. He must be after the ring and the stone. We need to put a fake clue in here and send him on a wild goose chase."

Phyllis thought it was a great idea, and Greg agreed. Greg mentioned there were a few trunks that had keys, and we should use one of them. I agreed. We needed to send him somewhere.

We tossed around sending him to a different country, but he may have known more than us so we agreed the note should lead to Florence. I pulled out my phone and started researching. We discussed several places and decided we would send him to a church. After a little more research, we decided on the 11th-century church called Abbazia di San Miniato al Monte, which was in Florence. We were looking at the paper. It was not brand new, but not too old. We need to find a piece of paper like this paper.

Phyllis asked for the paper. She looked closely at it, "Lillie wrote this. Check the desk for this type of paper."

I opened the desk and found nothing resembling it. Phyllis swiftly left the library, and we followed. She headed up to the desk Lillie had in her bedroom. We watched as Phyllis went through the desk.

I know I have seen this paper before, "she said as she rummaged through the desk.

Greg said, "What about the desk by the front door?"

We quickly made our way downstairs to the first floor. Phyllis started looking through it and still nothing. She sat there for a minute. She reached for a box on top of the desk. It was about four inches by four inches. As it was opened, it revealed the paper

Grandma used to write the note. She took a few pieces of paper and grabbed Grandmother's pen from the desk. Without saying a word, she moved to the dining room. Phyllis handed us each a sheet of the 4" X 4" paper. She asked us each to try and mimic my grandmother's writing by scribing the name of the church on the paper. Upon review of everyone's samples, we decided Phyllis was the closest to her handwriting.

Phyllis made herself comfortable before creating the fake clue we would later hide in the library desk. Greg told us he was going to get an iron key he saw in the attic. I hovered over Phyllis as she worked. When she finished, she turned to me and handed me the paper. I compared it to the real clue. They looked remarkably similar. I put both papers in front of her to see what she thought.

Phyllis said with pride, "Not bad, huh."

I told her she did a wonderful job. I headed back to the library with both notes. Greg was still in the attic. While we waited; I checked the desk for another secret compartment, but I did not find one. I heard Greg coming down the stairs and hollered at him to let him know we were in the library. He came in and handed me an iron key.

"I left the trunk unlocked in case you needed to get into it," he agreed the fake note was perfect.

I took a deep breath and put the key and the fake note in the secret compartment before putting it back on the desk. I placed the note in my mirror to ensure I did not lose it. Greg and I headed back downstairs to find out from Phyllis where we should leave the key for Mom to find it.

We found Phyllis folding clothes in the laundry room. She told us Phillip's jacket was on the chair by the piano. Put the key under the chair behind the back leg. She will think it fell out of his jacket. She told me to act like I was looking for the key when she gets home. I need to try and have Mom help me look.

Greg headed home and after I placed the key behind the leg of the chair, I helped Phyllis in the kitchen preparing stuffed pork chops for dinner until I heard the Cadillac come down the drive. I scurried to the drawing-room before she came in to act like I was looking for the key. When I heard Mom's heels in the hall, I picked up the sofa cushion and looked under the cushion.

The heels stopped in the foyer just outside the drawing-room, "Did you lose something?"

"I'm looking for Phillip's key. Do you know where he was sitting?" I asked.

Mom pointed to the chair by the fireplace. She took her heels off and put them on the stairs. "I will help you look. Phillip called me today asking about it and I assured him we were looking," she said as she looked around the bar.

When we finished searching the drawing-room, I asked, "Do you think he could have dropped it in the foyer or up in his room?"

"It's possible," she headed to the foyer and searched. I checked the desk area because it would force her to check the area by the chair and the piano. I turned around, and she was looking by the chair.

She looked as though she was going to move on to the piano, when I said, "Do you need help moving the chair?" I asked.

She went back to the chair, "No, I've got it."

"I will check the stairs," keeping her in my sightline as I pretended to look around.

She pushed the chair back toward the wall and still did not see the key, but when she pulled it forward, I heard a small clank. She pulled the chair away from the wall and looked behind it. "I've got it," she said enthusiastically.

"That's great! Phillip will be so happy. I felt bad when he said it was his dad's. It must have devastated him. I know how much this necklace and the mirror mean to me. "I said.

"I must call him and let him know we found it," she said as she picked up her phone to dial his number, "Phillip, I found your key," Mom stared at the key, "It was under the chair you had your jacket on." She listened to him for a minute before replying, "That sounds good. I will give you some dates when I get my schedule at work figured out."

As she was ending her call with Phillip, Phyllis called us to dinner.

At dinner, Mom informed us she would be out of town the following week and was heading to New Orleans for a conference. She was so excited as she told us everything that had happened at work.

Twenty

The next few days, Greg and I spent a lot of time together. We decided to go to Italy in a week. We need to discover the meaning behind the clue we found. We enjoyed going to Parkour every few days. On our runs, we have even begun jumping atop things or hurdling over them. Of course, Greg was doing flips and swinging on street signs while we ran around, while I was nowhere near ready for that.

We had a good workout at Parkour. Never could I have imagined doing Parkour. I pushed myself because I was becoming confident in my newfound strength, physically and mentally. Being able to leap from one object to another made me feel powerful. I fell a few times, but I picked myself up and tried it again.

As I ran for a hurdle, I put my left hand down and threw my legs over. I continued running and did the same action again on a higher hurdle, but instead of landing on the ground, I jumped to the next hurdle and landed on top. I could not believe I was doing so well. From the hurdle, I jumped to the next platform. The next jump was much farther away. I went for it. As I jumped, I realized I would not make it, but I calculated I could grab the edge of the structure and not break my neck. I reached out to grab the ledge. My left hand slammed into it and my left side collided with the wall. Holding the full weight with my right hand. My left hand lacked the strength to hold me and was hurting. I held on, knowing it was a long way down. Not wanting to fall, I gripped as long as I could until I could not hold my weight. I slid down the wall and fell on my butt and left hand.

A staff member came over to me and helped me up, "Hey there. I'm Gloria." The Hispanic woman was about 5'6", with dark curly hair. She looked to be in her twenties. "I saw you hit the wall. Follow me we need to get you some ice."

I could not believe how badly my hand was hurting. As we headed toward the entrance, I looked around for Greg. He was not in sight. She put me in a chair and told me she would be back. She darted way.

She returned with a small bag of ice and sat down next to me. "Is there someone I can call for you?" she inquired.

"Please page Greg Scrogham?"

She went to the receptionist to ask her to page Greg. I looked down at my hand. It was swelling.

"Greg Scrogham to the front please, Greg Scrogham to the front please," a deep voice said over the PA system.

Gloria sat back down beside me and tried to comfort me. When a handsome black man walked up and said, "I hear you had quite a fall. Would you like me to call an ambulance?"

"No, thanks. My friend Greg is here. He can take me." I adjusted the ice to a more comfortable position on my hand.

Greg walked right past me and went up to the front desk. I think the manager was blocking his view. The clerk pointed to me, and Greg ran over to me. I filled him in on what happened. The manager gave me some paperwork, and Greg and I headed to the hospital. I did not want to call my mom because she just started her new job, so I called Phyllis to let her know we were heading to the hospital. She offered to come, but I told her I was fine.

At the hospital, they informed me I fractured two of my metacarpal bones in my palm. They put a blue cast on my hand. It went about four inches past my wrist. I needed to wear the cast for four to six weeks. The doctor recommended acetaminophen for pain.

We headed home. Greg hung out with me for the rest of the day. He wanted to be there when Mom arrived in case; she had questions.

When Mom arrived, we told her everything that happened. She told me she was glad Phyllis and Greg would be with me next week to help me out if I needed anything.

The next few weeks were uneventful. Our trip to Italy had to be canceled because of my hand. I needed to be prepared for anything when dealing with the Granaldi brothers. Once my hand started feeling better, we started working out again. We just eliminated using my left hand until it healed. The sweating was making the cast incredibly itchy and smelly. I tried several things to stop the itching and to remove the odor including perfume and baking soda, but nothing really helped.

Mom informed me one morning that Phillip was coming back that weekend to celebrate my birthday. I could not believe she invited him. It was the first weekend she had off. I figured she was not working because it was my eighteenth birthday. I pictured myself spying on him, trying to find the lock on the desk. Secretly I hoped he would find the fake clue because it might mean he may not need to return to my home.

Greg promised me he would keep me company while he was in town. He was working on a side job. I did not know if I was going to get to see him before tonight. He was taking me out on a date. Greg did not tell me anything about it. *Where are we going? What should I wear?* I called Mechelle for suggestions, but she did not answer. Finally, choosing to wear white jeans, sandals, and a turquoise V-neck top with straps and ruffled sleeves that left my shoulder exposed. I curled my hair, put my makeup on, and headed downstairs.

Greg was on time as usual with a beautiful bouquet of Peach Roses, White Camellia, and Queen Anne's Lace. I thanked him for the flowers and Phyllis told me she would take care of them. As we walked out, I realized he looked handsome in his baby blue collared shirt and dark blue jeans.

We pulled up to Jeff Ruby's Steakhouse, and it looked expensive. As we walked in, Greg instructed me to remain by the door while he talked to the hostess. I looked at the beautiful chandeliers and decorations that adorned the room. It was very elegant with white tablecloths and napkins. The wooden floors were black and brown wood in a nice triangle pattern through the main walking area. Each table had a small bouquet. We followed the hostess to the back of the restaurant. I could not believe how beautiful the restaurant was. Busy looking around, I did not notice everyone that was sitting at the table until they all yelled happy birthday. My eyes moved in the direction of the hollering. I looked at the table and my mother got up and hugged me; I noticed Phillip was sitting next to her. *I am not letting you ruin my evening.* Barely acknowledging him, I moved my gaze to the table. The biggest surprise of the evening, Mechelle, was at the table.

I ran over and gave her a big hug. "I can't believe you are here!" I gave her another hug. I said hello to everyone else at the table before sitting down. Balloons were attached to my chair. From the left, around the table, it was Phillip, Austin, Greg, me, Mechelle, and mom. Greg and Mom had planned the evening.

Mechelle gushed, telling me she came early in the day, and Greg and Austin picked her up from the airport. They went on a shopping spree until dinner.

Greg added, "She was my side job. I dropped Mechelle and Austin off at the restaurant, and I ran home to change before picking you up. While I was home, I put Mechelle's luggage in my garage so you wouldn't see it."

The server came by and took our drink orders. Mom asked us to figure out what we wanted to eat. I think she was hungry.

I opened the menu and was in shock about the prices. Everything sounded amazing. Mom leaned forward to tell me to get whatever I wanted. I decided on the Petite Surf & Turf with Creamy Mashed Potatoes and the Classic Creamed Spinach. Mechelle told me she was not leaving until Tuesday. Mechelle and I spent most of our time talking with Greg and Austin, while Mom and Phillip chatted. *Where is Phyllis?* I could not help but wonder if Phillip was the reason, she did not join us. He probably talked Mom out of inviting her. The food came and everyone's meals looked amazing. I enjoyed my dinner. After dinner, Mom invited everyone back to our house for dessert.

Mom and Phillip rode back together, and the rest of us rode back in Greg's truck. Austin and Mechelle seemed to get along well. As we parked in front of the house, Mechelle said, "This house is beautiful."

Greg and Austin headed to Greg's house to get Mechelle's suitcase, while we headed into the house through the front door. I opened the door to reveal the foyer and staircase, Mechelle said, "Wow! This place is amazing."

I giggled, "This is just the foyer."

Mom and Phillip were in the drawing-room. I went over and thanked my mother for dinner. I cannot believe she picked up the entire bill. When we were in Florida, she would not have been able to afford this evening. Greg and Austin came in and joined us in the drawing-room. We were talking about how wonderful dinner was when Phyllis walked in.

I ran up to Phyllis and said, "Ms. Phyllis, I want you to meet my best friend Mechelle, and this is Austin. Ms. Phyllis is like family."

After acknowledging them, Phyllis said professionally, "Dessert is served."

Everyone went to the dining room, which was decorated with balloons from the restaurant and with so many gorgeous flowers. Everyone sat down and Phyllis served us coffee and hot tea. She came out with a beautiful lemon and blueberry cake with candied lemons that came across the top of the cake and down the side. Blueberries and icing flowers nestled beside the lemons. They placed two candles on the top of the cake. Everyone sang Happy Birthday, and as they sang, I watched the candle flicker and thought about what

I wanted to wish for. I took a deep breath and wished for my mother to find love, and I blew out the candles.

After dessert, I opened my presents. Austin gave me a gift card to Parkour, Phillip gave me a bottle of perfume, which I wondered if he hoped I would wear when I was spying on him because he would know it was me, but I would not be wearing any during his visit. Phyllis gave me a pair of running shoes, Mechelle gave me a framed picture of us together at the beach, Mom gave me a check for five hundred dollars, and Greg gave me a beautiful pair of earrings that complimented my necklace perfectly. After thanking everyone, I asked my mother where Phillip and Mechelle would be sleeping. She informed me Phillip would be in the guest room on the second floor and Mechelle could either have the guest room on the third-floor or she could stay in my room with me.

Austin, Greg, Mechelle, and I headed upstairs, and Phillip and Mom stayed downstairs, while Phyllis cleaned up. Austin brought Mechelle's suitcase up before I took her on a quick tour of the second and the third-floor. Once I showed her the third-floor room, she decided she would stay there and said it was because I toss and turn too much in my sleep. I think it was because the room is gorgeous. I was glad because I needed to spy on Phillip and if she were in my room that would make it difficult.

We hung out in the third-floor sitting room talking about everything going on in our lives. She decided she wanted to see me doing karate, so Austin decided he would join us in the morning too. They stayed until about 11:00 am and we walked them out. We went to my room and started talking about Greg and Austin. The door to my room was ajar. It allowed me to know when Phillip came upstairs. He went to his room about ten minutes after the boys left. I started acting tired, so Mechelle went to her room, and I shut my door and got ready for bed. I transported myself to the library, ensuring I was invisible. I waited to see if Phillip would show up. After twenty minutes of waiting on him, I felt my legs giving out. I needed to sit down. It was then I heard his door open and him walking down the hall.

He gently closed the library doors and began looking at the bookcases again. He rummaged through a lot of books. He tried moving the shelves before heading back to his room. It relieved me when he turned in for the evening.

The next morning, I dressed and headed up to Mechelle's room and found her still sleeping, so I woke her up and told her to meet me downstairs for breakfast. I walked into the kitchen and Phyllis was making us Crab Eggs Benedict with a side of fresh berries. I told her how I missed her at dinner. She wished she had been there.

I was making myself a cup of coffee when Mechelle came into the kitchen. "I need some of that please," she motioned toward the coffeepot.

We had breakfast with Phillip and Mom before they headed to Churchill Downs. We did not want to go. I informed her we already had plans. We headed over to Greg's garage where Greg and Austin set everything up for our workout. I put our towels down and I showed Mechelle what to do. The guys joined us.

After stretching, we headed out for a run. Austin could keep up, but Mechelle struggled. She grabbed her side and her pace slowed. I had a flashback of myself when I started this journey. We headed back to his house.

Austin worked with Mechelle, while Greg and I worked together. Once we warmed up, Greg asked Austin to spar with me, while he explained to Mechelle what was going on. "This needs to be even. Neither of you can use your left hands."

We got our pads on. Mechelle sat in the chair and watched as Austin, and I began sparring. Austin was being easy on me at first until he realized I was not without skills. I had learned a lot since I sparred with Greg's father, Andrew.

When we finished, Austin said, "You have learned a lot. I'm impressed." He turned toward Greg and joked, "Who would have thought Greg could be an excellent teacher."

Mechelle added, "I can't believe you can do this. It's amazing."

Twenty-One

We cleaned up and headed to the Mega Caverns for the Mega-Quest aerial rope course in the caves under Louisville. Unfortunately, as we were purchasing the tickets, they explained I could not go because of my broken hand. So, we took a tour of the caverns on the Mega Tram instead.

We learned a lot about the history of the caverns during the hour tour, and we watched as several people were zip-lining through the caves. By the time we finished the tour we were hungry, so we headed to the Recbar. I walked into the restaurant; It surprised me to see every wall had some type of video game. Austin showed us to the backroom, which had more pinball machines than I had seen in my entire life. There must have been sixty or more. What a unique experience this is. There was nothing like this in Palm Beach County. We sat down and ordered our food before playing games. I had the Cougar Bait Fish Tacos, and they were delicious. After we ate, we spent about an hour playing games. Austin and Mechelle were extremely competitive. We had so much fun with the video games and pinball; we did not realize we had been there for hours.

As we were trying to decide what to do next, Mom texted me. I told them I was going to call my mother and would be right back. I headed outside to call her.

I told her how much fun we have been having. I asked if she and Phillip were having a good time. She told me he was taking a nap. We talked for a few minutes more before I got off the phone. I texted Greg that I needed him to stall them.

I walked around the side of the building and stood behind the dumpster to transport to the library. When I arrived, I was so close to Phillip; I held my breath before slowly moving away from him. He was looking around the library and seemed frustrated. Phillip pulled the rug up and looked under it before he dropped it.

He picked up his phone and called someone, but I could only hear his side of the conversation. "I have been looking, I went through the attic in the middle of the night. There is nothing downstairs," he said with frustration in his voice.

I could hear the person talking, but I could not make out the conversation.

"I have been checking the library. I have even looked for a secret passage, I have gone through all the books." he paused as he turned and faced the desk. "Let me call you back," he said and hung up the phone.

Phillip's eyes fixed on the desk. He moved his hands along the decorative carvings on the front of the desk, before pulling on them. This continued as he worked his way around the desk. Phillip moved the chair and laid under the desk and inspected it. He looked at the floors underneath it and pulled on the top. His face said he was feeling defeated. He put the chair back and sat down, continuing his inspection of the desk. He even went through the things on top of it. I nearly took a step toward him to get a closer look, but I halted my movement when I heard a creak and immediately stopped moving.

Fortunately, Phillip did not notice because he looked like he may have just found the secret cabinet. After a good tug, he pulled the secret compartment out and placed it on the desk. The pride of his accomplishment gleamed on his face. He pulled the key out of his pants pocket and unlocked the secret compartment before leaving the key near the edge of the desk. Everything slides out of the compartment onto the desk. Phillip looked at the empty compartment. He did not notice he knocked the key onto the rug. After taking a deep breath, he picked up the paper and read it. He put the desk back together and picked up his phone and called someone. "I've got it. I need to find out what the note means, but we are one step closer." Practically skipping, he headed toward his room, leaving the key on the floor.

Who is he working with? He fell for our fake clue, and he'll be heading to Abbazia di San Miniato al Monte.

I became aware everyone must be wonder where I was; I returned to the dumpster at the Recbar. They stood outside, and it looked like they were looking for me. I snuck around toward the front door of the restaurant while they were out in the parking lot searching. I pretended to be coming out the door, and I hollered at Mechelle to let her know where I was.

"Where were you?" Mechelle asked.

"My mom called and when I went back into the Recbar I looked around for everyone but did not see anyone. I headed back to the bathrooms. I figured someone must be there. Several minutes passed before I headed out here to look for you. I don't know how I missed you," I explained.

We sat in the parking lot thinking about what we could go do. We tossed around several ideas and decided we would let Mechelle decide. She wanted to check out the mall. We headed there and walked in and out of stores, checking the latest sales. The guys looked rather bored but did not complain once. They spent a lot of time hanging out on benches outside of the stores. We finally drove around Louisville so she could see it. My stomach started growling. We headed out for a bite to eat. Everyone agreed to get a bunch of appetizers rather than get meals. We hung out at the restaurant for a while before the guys took us downtown. Greg took me over to a horse-drawn carriage. I looked back at Austin and Mechelle. Mechelle was smiling, and she grabbed Austin's arm and turned, and started walking in the opposite direction of us.

Greg helped me up into the carriage. As we rode around, enjoying the cool breeze of the night, Greg grabbed my hand and turned toward me with a smile. He was like a comfortable sofa you never wanted to leave.

"I want you to know, you're incredible. I've never felt so drawn to anyone," he said, looking like he had more to say.

Filled with emotions, his sweet words choked me up. I felt overwhelmed by my emotions and fought back crying tears of joy. My heart skipped a beat, "I feel the same way." *Please kiss me.*

He looked deep into my eyes, "Brooke, I love you." He stroked my hand.

"Greg, I love you too. You mean the world to me," I said, as he leaned in toward me as if to say, can I kiss you. I leaned in closer to him to let him know I wanted to be kissed. He moved my hair away from my face and kissed me. I felt frozen in the moment. His lips were so gentle. At this moment, I felt so connected to him. I did not want this moment to end. We held each other and kissed a few more times before the carriage came to a stop.

We looked around, Austin and Mechelle were sitting on a bench in the distance, talking.

As we walked over to them, I felt as though I was walking on a cloud. It was not until the ride home I realize I never told Greg about Phillip finding the secret compartment.

The next morning, while Mechelle slept in, I ran downstairs to see what was for breakfast. I noticed Phillip's suitcase at the front door. I cannot imagine he brought the suitcase down on his own. Surely, he had Phyllis up early to deal with it; I thought sarcastically. He was in the drawing-room.

"Good morning," I said, wondering if he would tell me anything, but he just nodded in my direction.

I thanked him for coming to the party and asked him if he knew if breakfast would be ready soon. He told me he was waiting for a cab because he had an emergency come up and had to head out.

That's right. You're going on a wild goose chase. "That's too bad. I hope everything is okay." Knowing he is leaving because of the fake clue he found.

"It will be," he said, as someone rang the bell. He picked up his suitcase and opened the door before turning and saying, "Please tell your mother I am sorry I had to go."

I nodded and waited for the door to close to show my enthusiasm for him leaving. I was so glad he was heading on a wild goose chase.

Over the next few days, I was finally able to tell Greg about what happened with Phillip; Mechelle and I got some cooking lessons from Phyllis; went four-wheeling with Austin and Greg on Austin's farm, and we went on a trail ride. Before I knew it, Mechelle was on her way home.

Twenty-Two

As the weeks passed, I started working out again after they removed my cast. I progressed to learning blocks, elbow strikes, which is a strike that uses the point of the elbow, and roundhouse kicks.

I also had started college and my professors seemed great. Greg and I did not have classes together, but we saw one another frequently at school. We often rode to the University together to save gas. When one of us was waiting on the other to finish class, we worked on our assignment until the other was done with their class. Mom had increased my allowance because of the extra expenses of school, and I think because she was making more money than she was making in Florida. I think her inheritance had something to do with it as well.

One morning, I was running late for school because I was up late working on a paper. I texted Greg to let him know I would see him at school. Mom was heading out of town again for her job today, so I gave her a quick hug goodbye as I ran out the door. Occasionally catching myself speeding, I had my mind on trying to make it to class on time. As I pulled into the parking lot, I realized I was going to have a tough time parking. I searched around and finally found a spot. I grabbed my backpack and started running to my class. There were several people late, but I seemed to be one of the few concerned about it. I ran past Miller Hall and was heading to Davidson Hall when I noticed a familiar figure sitting on a bench by the Life Science Building facing Davidson Hall. He seemed to pretend to read a newspaper, but I got a good look at him when he looked at someone walking in the building.

What is Phillip doing here?

He was watching a girl that looked similar to me. When he realized it was not me, he sat back and continued to pretend to read a paper. I needed to go another way to Davidson Hall. There were too many people around. I either needed to head straight to class and figure a way out of the building without getting caught or I would miss class. I could not afford to miss class, so I ran for the door.

I entered the class, apologized for being late, and took my seat. I sat there half-listening to my professor and thinking about why Phillip was in town when my mom was leaving. He must have known we sent him on a wild goose chase. I needed to figure out what he was planning.

I had a hard time concentrating on the professor and before I knew it; the professor dismissed us. As I skipped down the steps, I realized I stepped on a piece of gum. I needed to take the gum off my shoe. *Don't I have enough problems?* The restroom was near the entrance. Annoyed by the gum, I waddled my way to the restroom stall. The gum distracted me, and I had forgotten about Phillip for a brief moment.

I took a deep breath and focused. There were several people in the bathroom. It was not safe to teleport yet, so I waited until it sounded as though I was alone. This brought peace to me. It was safe to leave. I opened the mirror. The clue from the desk was still there. I put it in my bra because it would be too easy to lose it when I teleported. My focus was on thinking of a place near my next class to teleport, too. The hedges outside Miller Hall were perfect. I'll hide behind them and still make it to my next class on time. I glanced at my mirror to confirm I was invisible. I waited for the coast to be clear and returned visible. I popped out from behind the bushes; Phillip was still watching for me at Davidson Hall. He was pacing and headed into the building.

I could make it to class on time. The thought of meeting Greg for lunch after class filled me with sweet thoughts of him. Juliet, a new friend of mine from class, always walked with me to the quad. Juliet, a beautiful girl from Hawaii, moved here when her father's company relocated him. She is about 5'5", with amazing brown skin and dark hair that she often had pulled away from her face.

As we walked out of the building talking about our class assignment, I forgot about Phillip. When I remembered, I looked around, but I did not see him. Juliet's friend Jacob joined us as we continued to make our way to the Quad. Jacob is a tall slender man about 6'3", according to Juliet he is a wizard with computers. Jacob and I chatted a bit about his computer skills when it occurred to me, he might be helpful if I ever needed help with computer work. I spotted Greg on a bench. We continued walking when Juliet and Jacob invited us to join them. They typically sit under a tree for some shade. Knowing I needed to talk to Greg about Phillip, I politely told them no.

I walked up to Greg; I gave him a quick kiss before sitting down. He started going on about his professor when I interrupted him. I filled him in about Phillip and we both looked around to see if he was anywhere close to us. The relief of not finding him allowed me to enjoy my time with Greg. We ate our packed lunches and discussed the possibility of him figuring out we sent him on a wild goose chase. *Is Phillip dangerous?* That was yet to be determined, but we knew he was working with the Granaldis. We discussed reversing roles and following him. It would be hard with classes because neither of us could afford to miss a class. We also needed to get to Italy. We decided to head to Italy on Labor Day weekend. There is little time to prepare. I headed back to class, keeping an eye out for Phillip, but he was nowhere in sight.

When I finished for the day, I texted Greg, but he did not text me back. He must still have been in class, so I started heading out to my car. I was about to cross the road when the Granaldi brothers headed my way in their black Toyota Camry. Quickly making my way toward a group of people. I asked them for directions as I watched the Camry pass by me. The Granaldis were far enough for me to rush across the street. I made a beeline to my car, making sure I stayed down low and hid behind cars as I tried to keep an eye out for them. Before entering my car, I glanced around to make sure the coast was clear before I got in and locked the car.

I laid down, trying not to be seen. Attempting to text Greg, but still no response. Reminded of the conversation Greg and I had at lunch about needing to follow them. I pictured myself invisible and transported myself to the back seat of the Granaldi's car.

Tony yelled, "How could you lose her!"

"You didn't need to drive so far away before turning around. We could have turned down the next lane and waited for her to head to her car," Joseph told him.

Tony knocked Joseph upside the head. Joseph narrowed his eyes at Tony. Tony yelled at him, "Keep looking, we need to find her car."

When I remembered my phone was not on silent, I pulled out my phone when I heard a ring. I freaked out until I realized it was Tony's phone. I shut my phone off and put it back in my pocket.

"We lost her," Tony told the caller. He had his speakerphone on.

The person on the other end of the call said, "I'm at her car." He then sounded like he was telling them where my car was. That voice sounded like Phillip. *I still can't believe Phillip and the Granaldi brothers are working together.*

"She was here, and her backpack is still in the car. She had it with her earlier. Perhaps she went somewhere with her boyfriend. Keep driving and see if we can find either of them around here."

They continued driving around the University. When they were a hundred yards away from my car, I teleported back to my vehicle. When I arrived, I peeked out the windows to see if they were anywhere in sight before leaving campus.

Once I was off-campus, I turned my phone back on and noticed I had missed several calls and texts from Greg. I pulled into a drugstore parking lot and called Greg to tell him what happened. He told me he thought he was being followed. We both headed to the safety of our homes to figure out our next move.

I did not see anyone following me on my way home. When I got home, I told Phyllis what was going on and headed to my room. Greg showed up about ten minutes after me.

We decided we needed to be extra careful when dealing with Phillip and the Granaldi brothers, especially since they were working together. We prepared for Italy. I pulled out a pad and pen to take notes. We needed to go to the bank and get some euros. We did not know how long we would be there, but we would need money. I searched on my phone and found out that Fifth Third Bank would exchange the funds for us. What would we tell our parents? We needed a plan to explain where we would be because we could not tell them we were going to Italy for the weekend. We decided to acquire some spying devices online. I found a pen that was voice-activated and had a range of forty feet. That might come in handy. There were a lot of other useful tools, but they are all expensive. We determined the pen was the best investment, so I ordered it. I researched to find out what the weather would be like. It should be in the high seventies during the day and in the high fifties at night.

My phone alerted me to a text.

PHYLLIS: There is a car parked across the street and there are two men just sitting in it.

We jumped up and saw the Granaldi's car out front.

"I need to find out what they are saying," I said. Greg wanted to go with me, but I told him that would be perilous. He agreed, so I headed back to the backseat of their car.

"We could always break in and get the necklace," Joseph said.

"I have already told you Pop said we can't do that. By the time we got in and they discovered us, they could leave, and we would not know where they would be. Besides, Phillip said there are mirrors all over the house that will help with her transporting," Tony informed him. He picked up his phone and called Phillip with the speakerphone on. "We found them. It looks like they went back home," he said to Phillip.

"Brooke is smarter than she lets on. We need to find out what she found. Wait till everyone leaves and go through the house to see if you can find anything, but make sure there is no evidence of your being there and get out of the house before they get back. No one must see you." Phillip instructed. "Let me know when they leave. I will come over and help look."

We let Greg get the euros from Fifth Third Bank because they might figure out what we are doing if I went. Greg will carry everything valuable. I gave Greg the note from the desk to keep at his house just in case they caught me. We spoke with Phyllis and told her everything.

We asked her to do her shopping when we were home. Our weakest day would be Sunday. They could easily come while we were at church.

Our training got even more intense; we were now going to Parkour 4U several times a week because we wanted to make sure I was ready. I had learned to conquer that jump, and I was getting stronger every day. I couldn't believe this time next week we will be in Italy. Greg had the funds we needed, but we still waited for the pen.

Sunday morning, I dressed for church and glimpsed at myself in the mirror. I knew I was in great shape, but I could not believe how fit my body looked compared to when I first moved to Louisville. My muscles were so defined. I finished getting dressed for church and headed down to meet Mom and Phyllis. Greg was going to church with his parents.

At church, I sat there listening to Pastor Ellis speak about David and Goliath. The more I listened to the sermon, it occurred to me I am David and my battle with is Phillip and the Granaldis. They are my Goliath. The more I thought about Phillip and the Granaldi brothers, the more I wanted to see what they were doing in my house.

They must be there already. I excused myself, headed to the bathroom, and locked myself in the stall before teleporting to the hallway outside my room, ensuring I would be invisible. It sounded as though someone was in my room. I tiptoed over to the doorway to see who was there. Phillip was going through my drawers. I heard noises from upstairs and downstairs as well. I went upstairs to see what was going on. Tony was in my mom's room. He was hard at work looking through mom's things. I teleported downstairs and heard noises coming from the kitchen. *What would possibly be hidden in the kitchen?* Joseph was going through our refrigerator. He pulled out a jar of hot pickled okra and ate a couple before putting it back.

Phillip yelled from upstairs, "Did anyone find anything?"

Tony yelled, "Nothing yet."

I do not think Joseph heard him. He seemed more concerned with the food in the house as he was going through the pantry. I went into the foyer to see if they were going to say anything else. Tony walked past me in a huff. I followed him into the kitchen, and we found Joseph sitting on the stool eating the chicken strips that had been in the refrigerator.

"What are you doing? They can't know we are here. Do you not think they will notice their food missing?" he shouted. "Follow me." They both headed upstairs to the third-floor. I transported myself up there and saw they were heading into the attic. Greg and I had already searched it.

Phillip came in, "I've got nothing, what about you guys."

They told him there was nothing. They discussed going back to Italy to talk to their dad about the next step.

It had not occurred to me before, but we might run into them in Florence. We would need to be incredibly careful. The time got away from me, so I returned to the church. There was another lady in the restroom with me. I flushed the toilet and headed out of the stall to wash my hands and get back to my seat. Women started piling into the restroom. People were already leaving. I looked around for Mom and Phyllis but could not find them. I texted Mom to let her know I would be at the car.

Shortly after I made my way to the vehicle, Mom and Phyllis arrived and Mom asked, "What happened to you?"

"I am so sorry. My stomach was bothering me," I said providing another lie.

We headed back to the house. When we arrived, I noticed Greg was not back from church yet, but I did not see any sign of the Granaldi brothers or Phillip. As we walked into the kitchen, Phyllis pointed at some crumbs on the counter. Mom and I helped Phyllis get lunch ready.

As we were eating, Mom asked if Greg and I were still meeting my Florida friends in Atlanta. That is what we had told her so we could go to Italy. "I expect you and Greg will be on your best behavior," she shot me a look that said, I mean it.

They did a good job not disturbing too many things because no one noticed anything appearing different. I however noticed Phillip was not as neat as Tony must have been.

Over the next week, Greg and I did more research, and the pen arrived. We tested it out on Karen and found out she has a crush on a boy at school named Eric. Eric also goes to their church and plays on the school soccer team.

We were leaving on Friday after Greg's last class, but we still needed to figure out where to leave our car while we were in Italy. Our families thought we were heading to Atlanta. I packed a backpack because we wanted to travel light. We did not know where we would be sleeping. I threw a hoodie, a couple of shirts, a pair of shorts, and a couple of extra bras and panties in my backpack. I printed a map of Florence and put it in the front pocket of my bag. The only things left to pack were my toiletries. Greg is bringing the note and the recording pen with him.

Friday finally arrived.

We had brought our backpacks for Italy with us when we left the house to head to class. Greg and I went through our list to make sure we had everything. During class, I had a hard time focusing because I was thinking about Italy. I was excited, and I must admit a little terrified because we did not know what to expect.

Greg and I were to meet at my car and when he arrived; I was checking my bag one more time to make sure everything I needed was there. Greg tapped on the window. I let him in the car. Greg said, "My buddy Nick said we could park the car at his apartment because he had an extra spot."

We stopped by and spoke with Nick to let him know it was us using his spot. Nick was an attractive guy with short blond hair and blue eyes. They knew each other from Parkour. Greg told him we were taking a bus, so Nick dropped us off at the bus station. After he left, we walked down the road searching for an area without cameras that we could be unseen and teleport to Italy. We finally found a spot in some bushes behind an abandoned building.

"When we get there, we will be invisible. We need to be careful not to let anyone run into us. Once we find a spot, we can discreetly become visible again. We are going to arrive at the Archi Rossi Hostel. I figure we can stay there. It is not expensive and includes breakfast."

I pulled my mirror out, Greg grabbed my arm, and we were on our way to Florence.

Twenty-Three

We appeared behind the building. There were several benches and potted plants, and a stone walkway through the area. We hid behind the tree to make ourselves visible. It was 9:15 pm in Florence. We walked to the front door of the hostel to check-in. Giada, the woman checking us in, looked to be in her mid-twenties, had short dark brown air, short bangs, and her nose had a piercing with a ring. She seemed to ignore me and listen attentively to Greg. Greg explained there would be two of us and we would prefer a private room with two beds.

She said," No problem." Her fingers clicked on the keyboard for a few minutes." Passports.".

Did she say passports? I had not even thought about a passport. This is a problem. Frozen in place, I did not know what to say or do.

She explained tourists from outside Italy must provide their passports to stay in any hotel.

Greg leaned over the counter, and started flirting with the woman, "So, where around here do ya hang out?"

She provided some local places. None of which I could pronounce. She asked again, "I need your passports."

"Regrettably, someone stole my sister's purse while we were on the train. Is there anything ya could do for us? Perhaps refer us to a place we could stay where we won't need passports," Greg asked as he continued to flirt with her.

Sister?

"Our policy is not to let people stay without a passport," she informed us.

"Perhaps we could pay for two nights upfront?" Greg inquired as he pulled out his wallet.

She agreed. Greg paid her and told her he hoped to see her again. She played with her hair and smiled at him. As we walked to our room, I noticed a few people were in the common areas. Our room had two beds with a cabinet for our clothes. The beds were white metal beds with gold balls on top of the four corners of each bed. They had white sheets and blue bedspreads with large white flowers. Our room also has a small bathroom with a shower.

It was late in Italy; we didn't want to wander around a strange city in the middle of the night. I wanted to check out the Villa Dianella. I pulled out my phone and looked at the picture I found online of the estate. We locked the room before transporting ourselves to the field near the villa.

We arrived in the dark, we could see the villa in the distance with a few lights on. We quietly made our way toward the building. There were two couples at a wooden patio table with wicker chairs chatting. They seemed to be getting to know one another over a bottle of wine. We quietly moved closer to the building; we swiftly followed a couple who seemed a little intoxicated into the building. A man walked up to them and asked how they were enjoying their stay.

Is this a hotel?

We walked down a few stairs to another level, which had several sofas and chairs, black coffee tables with several coffee-table books about Italy and candles on them. We walked a little farther and noticed a pamphlet for Villa Dianella on a table. When no one was around, we quickly flipped through the pamphlet. It was a bed-and-breakfast.

We returned to the hostel to get something to eat. We will return to the villa tomorrow. We had dinner at Gustapizza, where we shared a Calzone Napoletano. It was delicious. We headed back to do some more research on the Granaldi Family.

Feeling guilty about lying to my mother about where I was, I felt it was important I keep my promise to my mother about our sleeping arrangements. After we got ready for bed, we kissed each other goodnight and we each slept in separate beds. I had a hard time getting to sleep because I could not shut my mind off, and it was only 7:00 pm at home, but here it is 1:00 am. We both knew we needed to get some sleep.

How can I go to sleep this early? Is Greg having a hard time falling asleep? I finally started focusing on my breathing, which relaxed me enough to doze off.

We both were up early and once dressed we headed to breakfast. There was a nice breakfast buffet, with croissants, yogurt, granola, eggs, and fruit. I got a coffee, yogurt, granola, and a banana, while Greg grabbed a coffee, eggs, a croissant, and some watermelon.

We were quietly enjoying our breakfast when a nice-looking man about 5'9" with a nice build and curly brown hair with blond highlights from the sun came over. "Hey there, I'm Wayne," he said as he sat down and joined us. That is when I noticed it looked like he slept in his clothes. He held his hand out for Greg to shake it, before extending it in my direction.

We introduced ourselves. "How are you enjoying Florence?"

"We just got here last night," Greg informed him.

"Americans. Cool. I'm from L.A. Well, I've been here for about a month. If ya need to know where anything is, I'm ya man. I play all over town," he informed us.

"You're a musician?" I asked.

"Yeah, I play the guitar and sing a bit. So where are you guys heading today? You should head to the Cathedral and the Ponte Vecchio for shopping. I will be at the Piazza della Signoria later today if you want to catch my show."

Breakfast wasn't bad. Wayne was nice, but we realized if we did not leave soon, he was going to talk until the next meal. We thanked him for his suggestions and told him we would try to catch his show.

We packed our things before we ate, so we grabbed our backpacks and caught a cab to the Villa Dianella. A lovely lady greeted us as we entered the building. She appeared to be in her forties.

She did not have makeup on and had her very curly hair in a ponytail. "Welcome to Villa Dianella," she said in a strong Italian accent. "How can I help you?" she asked as I read her name tag.

"Isabella, we are considering staying at your bed-and-breakfast. Would you mind if we looked around?" I asked.

"Yes, I will have Leonardo, take you on a tour," she said as she stared at my necklace. "What a beautiful necklace? Where did you find such a beautiful piece?" she asked.

"Thank you. It was my grandmother's?" I said as I caressed the stone.

"It is lovely," she said, turning and picking up the phone. She whispered to the person on the other end of the line.

I was looking around the front entrance. A man walked up wearing tan slacks and a white shirt. He appeared to be in his late forties or early fifties. As he was walking up toward us, Isabella motioned in my direction. He walked up to us, "I am Leonardo and who might you be?"

We introduced ourselves.

He turned to me, "My wife is right, that is a beautiful necklace. She tells me you received this from your grandmother. Would your grandmother's name be Lillie?"

Shocked he knew her name, I was not sure if I should answer. It was then I realized the stone was not warning me of any danger, "Yes, did you know her?" I asked.

Leonardo explained my grandmother would stay with them whenever she was in Florence. They had known her for years. They did not know of my grandmother's passing and offered their sympathy, and you could tell Isabella and Leonardo seemed upset by the news. He offered for us to stay at the villa at no charge because my grandmother paid to reserve a room for the year to ensure it was always available.

Odd. Why would she pay for a year in advance? She must trust them.

Greg and I looked at each other with a smile. That would be great. This place is much nicer than the place we are at. He took us up to a room, which had a queen-size bed with a small settee at the end of the bed. Two small tables with lamps were on both sides of the bed. A curtain came down from the ceiling, but it was open and pulled back to the wall on both sides of the bed. There was a full-length mirror and an armoire in the room.

"This was your grandmother's room. I would be honored if you stayed here. After lunch, most of our visitors will tour the area. I suggest you and I take a tour of the villa when most of our guests will be sightseeing. In the meantime, enjoy your stay," Leonardo said as he handed us each a key before leaving.

If it were not for the necklace not warning me, I might suspect he was not honest. Leonardo and Isabella, both made me feel comfortable. Greg and I put our backpacks down and looked around the room. The room was beautiful, and the view was amazing. We walked around the grounds. I enjoyed the romantic atmosphere and could see why my grandmother loved it here. Isabella found us and directed us to an outdoor table that was more discrete than the other tables. Leonardo pulled out my chair for me to sit in. Greg sat down next to me. Leonardo and Isabella joined us. A server came over and filled our water glasses and offered us some wine. We both turned it down.

Leonardo said, "You probably have a lot of questions for us. I should let you know your grandmother was a special woman. She would visit us regularly and would stay a few days before heading back home or onto another adventure. She has confided a lot in us over the years. I like to think that we helped her as much as she has helped us, but I know we got more out of the relationship than she did. She proved to us that one of our previous staff was stealing from us and it nearly broke us. Lillie recovered some of the money and jewelry that was stolen from us and our guests. Lillie was a blessing to us."

The server came back and dropped off our drinks.

Once he left, Leonardo continued, "We assisted Lillie with research and helped her keep some of her secrets safe."

"Secrets?" I asked. *Did they know about the Bloom of Dreams?*

"Lillie was our friend and trusted us, just as you can," Isabella said and took a sip of her wine before continuing. "We have something to show you, but we must wait for people to head into town for the day."

The server came back with soup for all of us, along with some toasted bread. I thanked him as I enjoyed the fragrance. The soup had dark greens, beans, and vegetables.

"This is Ribollita, enjoy," Isabella informed us.

The soup was thick like a stew. It was not like any soup I have eaten. "This is delicious," I said.

"We will always give you the privacy you need while you are here. If you need anything, please let us know and we will do what we can to assist you. If you want your room cleaned, please let us know. Your grandmother and I had an understanding, her room was only to be entered with her permission. Out of respect for her and because she would always pay us a year in advance, we respected her wishes. The last time she was in the room was about six months ago," Leonardo informed us.

That was about a month before grandma died.

Why was she here? Were the Granaldi family after grandma? If so, how at her age was she able to get away? Did she know what they wanted. The more I found out, the more questions I had.

Twenty-Four

We finished lunch and Leonardo said, "Please follow me." We followed him into the villa and down several stairways into a room with eleven extremely large barrels of wine lining the walls. At the other end of the room was a shelf with about thirty bottles of wine.

As we walked into the room, Isabella shut the door behind us. We heard the door lock. Greg and I looked at each other. *Why did she lock the door?* The stone did not warn me of any danger.

Leonardo walked to the shelf with the wine bottles. "Brooke, is it okay if Greg stays here while I show you something of your grandmother's?" Leonardo asked.

I looked at Greg, "He and I have no secrets."

Leonardo asked us to step back. He pulled the shelf away from the wall, "Please head down the stairs. I will wait for you here to ensure the secrecy of the room."

Greg and I looked down a dark stairwell, wondering if we should enter. Leonardo hit the light switch just inside the stairwell. We could now see the pathway to another room.

I made my way down the few steps; the small room contained a full-size bed, a bookshelf with several books, a sink, a toilet, and a small table with two chairs, a small refrigerator, some food, and a couple of pictures on the wall one of which was of my mother, my grandmother and myself. I remember Phyllis taking the picture at Christmas a few years ago. We explored the room and discovered a safe behind a picture.

Greg pulled out the note we found in the desk for what could be the combination. He tried the numbers 17 23 13 20 18 to see if they would open the lock. Greg grabbed the handle, "Cross your fingers." He pulled the lever to open the safe.

We both looked at each other with excitement in our faces as the safe door opened. Greg moved out of the way to let me get the contents of the safe. He looked over at me, "Would you like some privacy?"

Without hesitation, "No, you should stay." I desperately wanted to see the items in the safe but realized it may contain my grandmother's deepest secrets. *Do I really want to know them?* I was not even sure the items in this safe were meant for me. The curiosity got the best of me. I reached in and found a floor plan of an extremely large home or building, a key, a piece of paper with an address on it, and a sealed envelope with my name on it. I handed everything but the envelope to Greg, and I immediately opened the envelope and noticed a long letter and knew it was my grandmother's handwriting.

    My dear Brooke,

      By now you have discovered the Bloom of Dreams has many gifts others will try to obtain. You are now its protector. In the event you are unable or unwilling to protect the stone, you must find an ancestor to take your place. Knowing you as I do, I am sure you have accepted your fate to protect the stone. You must have met Leonardo and Isabella if you are reading this letter. I trust them with my life. They know about the stone and the importance of protecting it. The room you discovered the letter in, is a safe room. If you ever need to hide someone or something, this is a safe place.

      Leonardo and Isabella had to spend nearly a week hiding in this room once when the Granaldi family hung around the villa because they suspected I was staying in the house. They also hid Phyllis there once to keep her safe. If you need anything, ask them. They do a lot of research for me. Leonardo and Isabella have a trust set up for you. They are the trustees. The trust will continue to cover the cost of my room, which is now yours. If you need anything, let them know and they will get it for you. This is the only way I could have your mother not get suspicious about the amount of money you inherited.

      You have probably already discovered the Granaldi family and Phillip Davis, my brother's son, are dangerous and I suspect they may be working together to get the stone. What you do not know is why they want the stone. Our family has protected the stone and its cradle for over a century. Anthony Granaldi II stole them from us many years ago. We could retrieve the stone but were unsuccessful in getting the cradle. They were using the stone to commit crimes. Your primary job is to protect the stone, but you must also try to stop them. They want the stone because it will allow them to get in and out of places easily to steal valuable items, which they then sell in the black market. I believe they are using the funds from these sales to finance other crimes.

Regarding Phillip, I have not figured out what he wants the stone for, but he is a lot like my brother, John. It is my fault they know about the stone because I told John about it not too long after I inherited it.

The Granaldis still have the cradle they stole from us; it's called the Bloom's Cradle. The cradle will make the stone even more powerful, which means the stone cannot fall into their hands. I do not know what powers it holds, nor have I been able to find it. I suspect it is at Anthony Granaldis III home in Florence. I have provided you a key and address, along with a floor plan of his home. I have been to their home many times but could not locate the cradle. I marked the floor plan with areas I have searched.

Do whatever you can with the Bloom of Dreams to help people and try to find the cradle. I trust you with this gift. I love you with all my heart. Stay safe.
Love,
Grandma

We put everything from the safe under our clothes and in our pockets before exiting the room. When we got to the top of the stairs, I gently knocked, and Leonardo opened the door.

"I hope you could find what you were looking for," Leonardo said as he closed the door to the secret room.

"Yes, thank you. My grandmother provided me a letter that explained how important you are to her and how I can trust you and Isabella," I said trying to push back the paper that was pushing my shirt forward.

"We need to leave because Isabella has a tour soon of the wine cellar," he informed us as we headed out of the cellar. I knew we could not teleport back to our room because someone may have seen us come into the cellar. When Isabella opened the door, the two couples we saw enjoying wine the night before were chatting. Isabella smiled at us as we walked out of the room to allow her to start her tour. We thanked Leonardo and told him we had some work to do. We headed back to our room to get a better look at the items from the safe.

Once in the room, I locked the door. We put everything on the bed. I looked over at Greg feeling thankful because I knew I could trust him and now I needed his help to stop the Granaldi family and to find the Bloom's Cradle. We looked over the floor plans. The home was three stories. It contained the first and second floors and a basement. I took a deep breath and slowly exhaled. I needed to calm down and focus. We began studying the plans and discussing what our next move should be. I could not help but feel my grandmother must be watching over us. I looked over at Greg and without saying a word, I smiled. *We are really doing this.*

Twenty-Five

We took a cab to the address my grandmother provided, driving past it I took in everything I saw. The house sat away from the road. With me having the image in my mind, we can return later.

The driver took us to Piazza della Signoria to see Wayne play. It was easy to find him because of the crowd. After enjoying a few songs, we understood why he had a large crowd. I dropped a few euros in his guitar case before heading to the hostel.

We had already paid for two days and could still use the room. Greg did not want me to go by myself, so I agreed to let him tag along but reminded him, despite being invisible, it was still important that we remain quiet.

From our room, we teleported to the front yard of the Granaldi's home. We walked toward the front of the house. There were several cars parked in the driveway. As we got closer to the house, we slowed our pace and kept to the grass to make sure we were quiet.

The first floor was about four feet above the ground, which made it difficult to look in the windows. We proceeded to the backyard.

The back of the house had double doors that led to an exercise room. We looked to see if there was anyone inside the house before trying the key. This was not the right lock. I looked in the window and we teleported inside.

We did not hear anyone as we entered the home. Greg grabbed the floor plans from his backpack. We reviewed the map to confirm the rooms my grandmother had searched. My grandmother covered most of the second floor and a few rooms on the first floor. It does not appear she made it to the basement. We stood in the exercise room with the backyard behind us. We could see three doors in front of us. We went left to work our way around the basement.

We found ourselves in the recreation room. There were several dark brown leather couches and chairs throughout the room. The room had hardwood floors with large area rugs. There was also a large bar in the back of the room with six bar stools. We searched the room, checking every drawer and cabinet to see if we could find anything about the Granaldi family and to find the Bloom's Cradle. Behind the bar was a door to a wine closet. Greg and I both went through the closet together. We even pulled on the shelves to see if any of them would move, but we found nothing. We headed to the game room, which was a circular room in the corner of the house. There we found a round wooden table with a black felt center. The outer edge of the table had spaces for poker chips and drinks. There was not much to check in this area other than the table. Since we found nothing, we moved on.

There are double doors on the opposite wall of the bar, which led to a mudroom. Just next to the mudroom was a reading room. We spent a lot of time checking all the books. As we exited the room to our left, we discovered stairs to the first floor. We stayed on the basement level. Next to the stairs, we found a closet with a few jackets and shoes. Behind the bar was a short hallway with several doors. The first door on the left was a closet. This closet had some umbrellas and several labeled keys hanging on a key rack. Next to that closet was a bathroom. The end of the hall had a door. We carefully opened the door to discover the garage.

I told Greg we should continue in the house first. The key did not unlock the door across from the bathroom. We continued down the hall. It widened in the center of the home. This area contained a circular stairway leading to the first floor.

As we reached the next set of doors to our left, a humming sound like an elevator grew louder. We froze in our steps and looked at each other to figure out what we should do. I was scared and felt like I could not breath. We moved away from the door. The door opened. A maid stepped out of the elevator. She was overweight and was wearing a black dress with short sleeves that had a white collar with black trim on the bottom.

She was walking toward us but stopped across from the circular stairwell and opened the doors. We tiptoed over to the area to see what was inside. It was a laundry room with a workbench and some tools and cleaning supplies. She began folding clothes. Just as I motioned for us to move on, the elevator hummed again. We quietly moved away from the doorway. This time a butler exited the elevator. He was wearing a nice suit. His hair was graying on the sides of his head. He entered the laundry room, and we witnessed him grab the maid around her waist and kiss her on the neck.

She said, "Well hello." She turned around and started kissing him. Greg and I looked at each other and knew we needed to move on. We headed down the hall to the other side of the house. The next set of double doors led to an office. This might lead to something. They set the room up with multiple computer stations. We checked and still found nothing. It was getting late, so we headed back to the hostel, grabbed our backpacks before heading back to the villa.

When we arrived at the villa, we unpacked and marked the map with the rooms we had checked before heading downstairs for dinner. Isabella was talking to a staff member as we came down the stairs. When finished with her conversation, she asked us how Florence was. We told her how beautiful it was. She informed us that dinner would be at 9:00 pm.

As we were talking, I noticed everyone was wearing business casual type clothes. I looked at Greg and myself and we look like we had been out hiking. Neither of us brought anything appropriate for dinner, so I asked Isabella if she could help. She told me the unclaimed items box might have something for us. She took us to a room that was used by the staff. We found a nice dress for me, and Isabella loaned me some sandals to wear with it because I only brought sneakers. Greg had dark jeans but did not have a nice shirt. There were several wrinkled shirts. Nothing appropriate for dinner. She got one of Leonardo's collared shirts for him. He did not have a choice but to wear his sneakers.

We went to our room got ready for dinner as quickly as possible. When ready I exited the bathroom, Greg looked at me and told me how beautiful I looked. The casual country-style dress had a tiny black-and-white checkered pattern. It was a smidgen too big, but it had ties that allowed me to tighten it some around my waist, which made it difficult to tell that it was too large. We headed down for dinner.

It was a beautiful night, so they were serving dinner outside. As we walked outside, a cool breeze drifted by, and Italian folk music played. I followed the sound of the music and noticed a man playing an acoustic guitar and a couple was slow dancing. Greg held his hand out and asked me to dance. We made our way next to the dancing couple. I slid my right hand into his left hand, and he gently laid his right hand on my waist. I placed my left hand on his shoulder. As he held me, I felt myself melting in his arms. This was such a romantic moment. The lights in the trees cast the perfect amount of light. My body tingled. I stopped thinking about the Granaldi family and the Bloom's Cradle. I let myself enjoy this moment. As the song ended, he took his hand from mine and placed it on my waist. He looked into my eyes. It felt like he was looking at my soul. I was under his spell, and nothing could pull me away from him. My heart fluttered.

Greg stopped dancing and placed his hand against my cheek. His thumb brushed my skin, "I love you." before kissing me.

We walked over to get a table and the host sat us at a table for six. We sat down and said hello to everyone. Thankfully, everyone spoke English fairly well. The couples appeared to be in their thirties. The server filled our water glasses before asking us what we would like to drink. The lady sitting next to me asked what it was like in America. I explained, "I am not that familiar with Italy, but I have noticed a few things in the short time I have been here. In America, we tip our servers for serving us and we eat much earlier than Italians."

The server brought out our drinks and liver pate for us to enjoy as our first course. Before leaving, he asked us if we would like fish, beef, or vegetarian for dinner. Greg and I both got the fish. He seemed a little skeptical about eating the pate; I have had it several times with my grandmother. Once he saw I was enjoying it, he tried it. Greg widened his eyes wide before he smiled and nodded.

The other couples seemed to know one another and were talking about the sites they ventured out to during the day. Greg and I talked about things we would like to see, knowing we would not see them on this trip.

My phone vibrated. I looked down to see it was my mother. I excused myself from the table to call her. She asked me if I was having a good time. Nearly telling her we were about to have dinner when I remembered it was only 3:00 pm at home. I told her we had been site seeing and were heading back to get ready for dinner. Promising to try to call her the next day, I ended the call.

I was walking back to the table and noticed the meal was being served. They served us Salted Cod with tomatoes, onions, and rosemary with garlic bread, roasted potatoes, and green beans. Everything tasted so fresh. The chef was a genuine artist. Greg seemed to enjoy it as well. For dessert, we had Schiacciata Alla Fiorentina, which was a sweet soft pastry with a bit of an orange flavor. They topped the pastry with powdered sugar. After eating it, Greg leaned in toward me with a napkin and wiped powdered sugar from my mouth. I blushed.

After dinner, we headed back to the Granaldi's home. We returned to the hallway outside of the office in the basement. We walked to the next set of double doors. Before entering the room, we listened to see if anyone could be heard.

Not a single noise came from the room, so we entered. It appeared to be a guest room because there was nothing in the dresser or nightstand. The closet had some extra blankets and pillows. The bathroom was bare as well. When we finished, we went across the hall to the only other door in the area.

We listened, and again I could not hear a single sound. We walked in to discover a large room with a swimming pool, a few chairs, some benches, and on the other side of the room, in the far corner, was a hot tub. I noticed a door to the right of the pool. We headed to the door and found a bedroom with a half bathroom. We searched the room and again turned up nothing except a small spiral staircase that led up to the second floor. It surprised me it did not stop on the first floor. We were nearly done searching the basement level.

We headed up the spiral staircase to the second story. When we arrived at the top of the stairs, there was a door. We opened the door and found ourselves in a closet. As we looked around, it appeared we might be in Anthony Granaldi III's master bedroom closet. We made our way to the next room, which was a grand bathroom.

We exited the bathroom to what appeared to be a private study just off the master suite. It was too dangerous to walk around the house with everyone home, so I turned the pen on to make sure it would record everything said in the room and I placed it under the nightstand next to the bed. In the search of the study, we found a personal computer, but neither of us was a hacker. We moved to the other side of the suite. I continued searching the drawers and Greg focused on the sitting room.

The door in the study's area flung open, creating an enormous noise. I tried to make my way to Greg, but I could not because he came in so quickly.

"I can't believe they came back here! Must I do everything myself," the man said as he entered the room, I was in. I looked at him, I recognized him from the picture I saw when I was researching the Granaldi family. This was Anthony Granaldi III, and I was presuming the large Italian lady behind him must be his wife, Maria. "We must get the stone. How difficult is it to rip it off some teenager? It is not like they are dealing with Lillie. Lillie had lots of training. This kid knows nothing. She probably does not even know what she is wearing around her neck." He stripped his collared shirt off to reveal a white tank top t-shirt.

Maria was taking off her jewelry and said, "They are trying, dear."

Anthony reached down to take off his shoes when I noticed the ring on his right hand. *The Bloom's Cradle!* He was wearing it. I stood there hoping he would take it off, but he did not. I slowly made my way over to Greg as they continued getting ready for bed. Once they seemed to have ended their conversation for the evening, we headed back to the Villa.

We discussed how we could get the ring. We did not want to kidnap him to get it off his finger. The only way we could get it and him not know it was us was to drug him, but what would we use and how would we get him to take it. We slept on it. Greg took the couch at the end of the bed, and I took the bed.

Twenty-Six

We rose early and headed down to grab some coffee and a quick breakfast. They had several types of bread with butter and jam, and a bowl of fruit. Although simple, the meal was delicious. We returned to our room to teleport to the Granaldi's home.

We arrived invisible in the basement hallway by the garage. Our goal was to get into the two rooms we could not get into before. When we arrived, two maids were talking; in the room we needed to search and the other was in the doorway. They were discussing the Granaldis.

"I know they don't let us know too much about what they do, but there's something about this family that leads me to believe they are not to be trusted. As soon as I find another job, I'm leaving," the one in the room said.

The maid in the doorway said, "I don't care what they do, they pay well. Come on, we need to get going. I'll get the elevator." She walked toward the elevator. The lady in the room finished making her bed and while she did, we stepped into the room and out of her way until she left.

Once she left, we started searching. We found her ID; her name was Sofia Grieco. Other than discovering her name, we found nothing. The other room remained locked.

We decided to sneak upstairs to see if we could overhear anything. When we reached the landing on the first floor of the large circular stairwell at the center of the home, we were in the vestibule. The doors to the left and right of the front door were open. One door led to the study and the other to the formal dining room. No one was in either room. We went into the dining room and looked around and again turned up nothing.

I looked in the study so I could return another time, but we did not search the room because there were too many things to search for, and everyone should be getting up soon. Noises came from the area of the kitchen. We walked out of the dining room toward the sounds using the door nearest the kitchen. Directly across the hall appeared to be a playroom of some sort. *Perhaps Anthony had grandkids.*

Just past the playroom was the kitchen and the living room. There was a lady preparing breakfast. Sofie walked in and took some dishes to the dining room and made a second trip for some food. The lady making the breakfast brought some coffee and juice to the table. We headed to the vestibule to listen in on their breakfast conversation.

We waited a few minutes, Tony and a lady with a young girl came in. The girl appeared to be about five. Sofia entered and put a towel on a chair before placing a booster seat on it. Tony's wife put the child in the chair. She poured coffee for Tony and herself before sitting between the child and her husband. Joseph arrived looking hungover. He sat down across from Tony. From the other room, Maria said something to the staff, but I could not make out what she was saying. Their father and Maria came in and sat at the ends of the table. Maria kissed the girl. Anthony said grace. Everyone let him get what he wanted before they serve themselves.

Maria was helping the child putting jam on the bread. She started informing everyone about the events for the day, "After church, everyone will come back for lunch. I invited a few people from our congregation over. I have informed the staff to have lunch set up outside. Everyone needs to hurry and get ready to leave soon. The staff will attend an evening mass tonight so we will eat out."

This was splendid news. This would give us plenty of time to search the house.

We patiently waited for them to leave. Once they left the staff was either in the kitchen or busy setting things up outside. We went to the study and began rummaging through the room. We made sure we were extremely quiet because the doors were open, and we did not want anyone to discover us. The study had two doors like the dining room. One led to the vestibule and the other to the elevator. We found nothing.

Across the hall was a half bathroom. The last room at this end of the hall was the library. We searched the other rooms because they kept the door to that room closed. Because of the library's location, we could search it when people were home. We headed down the hallway and passed the dining room to what appeared to be a music room. There was a couch, a piano, and musical instruments adorned the walls. Just off the music room was a sunroom with two couches and several chairs. Again, we discovered nothing.

I am getting discouraged. We moved to the next room, the mudroom. We could not search the living room and the kitchen because of the staff, so we headed to the second floor.

The first room appeared to be a guest room, with a bathroom and a small closet. There was also a sitting area. Just down the hall was an enormous suite. As we looked around, it appeared to be Joseph's room. We found several weapons: a couple of knives, a handgun, and a shotgun. We also found a notepad. Not wanting to take the time to read it, I took a picture. This room had a patio and a larger bathroom.

We went passed the enormous staircase to the first room on the left. Another unused guestroom. The last room was the child's bedroom. It was a beautiful princess theme with a play area. We went to the only remaining room at this end of the hall. Once we entered, it was apparent we were in Tony and his wife's room. There were more weapons and what looked like a journal. If we took it, he would know. I snapped a few pictures of the last few pages to look at later. This room was the opposite floor plan of Joseph's room. We moved on to the upper living room, which was on the other side of the staircase.

We headed back to Anthony's room and started going through his closet. They mounted a safe on the wall. In our rush to get back to their house, we realized we left the key at the villa. We stayed and continue looking. We could come back later and find out what was in the safe if we had a key.

They would arrive soon. We headed back to the basement to see what we could find. We discovered a sauna next to the exercise room. It was not on, which made it easy to look around it. Greg sat expressing his frustration with not finding out more information and apologizing for forgetting the key.

As he was sitting there, he kept staring at the paneling. He jumped up and pushed on the it. It opened and revealed another safe that needed a combination. *We needed to get the combination.* As we exited the sauna, we looked outside to see if people were arriving yet. The family was back with guests.

We needed to know what everyone was saying. Greg started following a staff member outside to see if we could discover valuable information. I followed. We split up to cover more ground.

As we walked outside, I noted how beautifully decorated their yard was. There is a large water feature in the center of the patio. The patio had light-colored bricks that complimented the home. There were several sitting areas with dark wicker sofas and chairs with light-colored cushions. There are dark wood coffee tables that complemented the furniture. The staff has set up a large table with white linens under a trellis that created a stunning green canopy above the table. I hung around Anthony, while Greg checked on Joseph and Tony.

Anthony sat talking to a man about the same age as him. "What is the status of the Le pigeon aux petits pois?" Anthony asked the man.

"We might have a buyer. He would like to meet us next weekend about it. He wants to meet in Paris," he informed Anthony.

"No, it's too dangerous. We meet in Italy," Anthony snapped at him. "Did you tell him the price?"

"Twenty million," he said, as a few of the other guests sat down next to them. I looked over at Greg. He was trying to tell me something. I think he is trying to say he cannot understand what they are saying. I had forgotten without the Bloom of Dreams he could not understand their language.

Once the other people sat down, the conversation regarding Le pigeon ended. After they finished eating, the man left. I was standing behind Anthony and my stomach growled. He turned around to see who it was. He stared right at me. I knew he could not see me. Despite that, my blood drained from my body. He turned back around and appeared to make eye contact with Joseph, who headed over to see what his father wanted. I moved out of my spot and moved to his left.

Joseph asked his father what he needed, and he motioned for him to move in closer. Anthony whisper, "I'm pretty sure Brooke is here and knows how to use the stone."

Anthony looked around. When I thought he was not looking, I made my way over to Greg. I saw Joseph walking over to Tony. He must be telling him I am here. I pulled out my mirror and Greg grabbed my arm. I transported us to the Villa.

Twenty-Seven

As soon as we arrived, I told Greg what I had overheard. They knew I was there. I called the front desk and asked Isabella if Leonardo could come to my room. I explained to Greg we needed Leonardo's help.

A few minutes later, there was a knock on the door. I opened the door and invited Leonardo in. "I know we don't know each other, but my grandmother trusted you with her life, so I trust you. My Grandmother told me if I needed anything, I could ask you and you would do what you could to help me. I believe the Bloom's Cradle is on Anthony Granaldi's hand. He does not take the ring off. I need to drug him and be able to get the ring off without him seeing me, and I want to make sure I used a drug will not harm him. I also need help to find out what Le pigeon aux petits pois are. All I know about it is it is worth a lot of money. We also need two small cameras. Can you help us?"

He told me I am more like my grandmother than he originally thought. He told us he could help us with the things we needed, but the drug might take some time. Greg and I went down to get something to eat and talked about what our next step would be. We needed to try the key in the safes and the combination. *I hope we can get both safes open.* After we ate, we went back to the room and search the internet to see what we could find out. Isabella provided us my grandmother's laptop that she had been holding on to for my grandmother.

Greg and I researched Le pigeon aux petits pois. What we found out is it's a Picasso painting from 1911. The name translates to Pigeon with Peas. It was one of five paintings stolen from a museum in Paris in 2010. The questions started coming; *Did the Granaldi family steal it? Who did they steal it from? Did they purchase it and are they now trying to sell it?*

We researched drugs, and we found a few that would work, but one stood out because it would cause sleepiness, relaxation of the muscles, and would make a person forget what happened. Rohypnol could be up to twenty times stronger than valium. We searched for Leonardo to tell him what we discovered.

Isabella was on a call at the front desk when we arrived. We waited for her to finish her call, before asking where Leonardo was.

She told us he was in their room, which was located just off the front entrance on the first floor. We knocked on the door and Leonardo seemed surprised to see us when he opened the door and invited us in. Their room was a little bigger than our room, and it had a sitting area. We sat in the sitting area and told him about the painting and Rohypnol. He said he had also discovered Rohypnol and had someone working on getting it for us.

Leonardo handed me a small box, "There are two small cameras with batteries." He explained he had them because my grandmother had needed them a few times. I opened the box to find two pinhole lenses and according to Leonardo, they both had mini-DVRs inside them. He explained we would need to retrieve the camera to see the video. Greg seemed confident the camera would work. "I think we can easily hide this in his closet, but we will need to hide the camera behind the paneling in the sauna, making sure the camera has a view of the safe. I will need some tools to do that," Greg told Leonardo. "If the key works on the closet safe, we can use the camera somewhere else in the home. Perhaps to have a view of his laptop," he added. Leonard asked Greg to go with him to get the tools he would need. I left and headed outside to get some sun until it was time to leave.

With the sun in my eyes, I moved a chair from one of the outdoor tables to a sunnier area. I sat there going through my phone and called Mechelle. I could tell when she picked up the phone, I had woken her. I could not tell her anything, but she knew what I had told my mother and she will cover for me. She tried to get me to tell her why I was lying to my mother, but I explained I could not tell her.

I saw Greg coming, so I quickly ended the call. He explained to me he got everything he thought he needed to put the camera in the sauna. I was eager to get back to see if the key worked. We decided we would grab something to eat before we left because of what happened at the Granaldi's lunch. We headed in to see if Isabella could help us get something to eat. She took us into the kitchen to talk to Chef Giovanni.

Chef Giovanni was an attractive man that appeared to be in his thirties. Isabella explained to him we needed him to prepare us a sandwich or something. He made us Italian Ciabatta Sandwiches, which had ham, salami, roasted red and yellow peppers, basil, arugula, olive oil, and balsamic glaze. As we ate it, I could also taste a hint of rosemary. It was delicious.

We headed back to our room because Greg needed to put the tools in his backpack. He removed his clothing from the backpack to make room for the floor plans, tools, cameras, and the key in the backpack. We headed back to the Granaldi's because we did not know when they would leave for dinner. We turned our phones to silent. Rather than use the compact mirror, we used the full-length mirror in our room to transport. I envisioned the sauna; we could easily see there was no one in the room. We stepped through the mirror, but before Greg got to work on installing the camera, I looked out the window to see if anyone was in the hallway. The coast was clear, so I stepped out into the hall. I went to see if anyone was in the pool area and the room just off the pool.

It appeared this area was clear also, so I went to the exercise room and saw no one. I went back to the sauna to inform Greg no one was around. He carefully removed some of the paneling from the wall across from the safe. Greg handed me his phone, which was open to the app he found that worked for the cameras. He positioned the camera according to my directions to ensure it aimed the camera at the safe. Once it was in place, he put the panel back. I looked to see if the camera could easily be located. It was difficult to find. I would not have noticed the small hole in the paneling for the camera if I did not know where it was. Greg did an excellent job. It took a little longer than we anticipated, but it was working. We cleaned up everything to make sure there was no evidence of us being in the room.

We headed upstairs through the small spiral stairwell that led to Anthony's closet. Even though we tried to be as quiet as possible, we notice a slight clanking coming from the backpack. Greg put the backpack on the ground and took off his shirt. He wrapped his shirt around the tools to prevent the clanking. He gently jiggled the backpack to confirm the problem was fixed. It was, so we continued up the stairwell.

We arrived at the top of the stairs and listened to see if we could hear anyone. I slowly opened the door and made my way into the closet. Greg left the door open. I presume for a quick escape if needed. We will also hear anyone coming up the stairwell.

I stepped into the bathroom and slowly made my way to the empty bedroom. I returned to the closet and caught a glimpse of myself in the mirror. I was visible. I had forgotten to make us invisible. It did not appear anyone was in the house, so I decided not to worry about it.

Greg handed me the key and said, "You should do the honors."

I placed the key in the safe. As I was turning the key; I felt the adrenaline flowing through me with excitement. The safe opened. It contained a couple of books, passports for Maria and Anthony, and some legal papers.

I took the first book out, it appeared to be a log of some sort. There was a list of items, a value, and some entries had notes next to them. I held it up for Greg to take pictures of a few of the pages.

The second book appeared to be contacts, which included addresses, phone numbers, along with some other information. He took a few pictures. We agreed everything should remain in the safe. So, I put everything back as I found it before locking it. Greg grabbed the pen from Anthony's side of the bed. Greg placed the second camera on a picture and aimed it at Anthony's computer. He had me sit in the chair to adjust the angle to see the screen better. Taking into consideration that Anthony was a much larger person than I was, he lined up the camera.

We headed out the master suite through the door by the large circular stairwell. We were cautious and headed down the hall to the library. As we walked, it appeared we were alone in the house. We went into the library and closed the door behind us just in case someone came home. Greg worked on one side of the room, and I worked on the other. We both found many books on valuable artwork. We had been searching for a while. The room was vast, nearly the size of the master suite.

Greg told me he was going to the bathroom down the hall and would be right back. I barely acknowledged him because I was focused on the area I was searching, making sure I checked for hidden compartments, when I heard a few thuds coming from the hallway. *Oh, no!* It sounded like a fight in the hallway. *I forgot to make us invisible.*

I could not believe I forgot to tell Greg. I opened the library door to find Joseph and Greg fighting. We could not transport right now. Greg had Joseph pinned down and told me to run. Greg's backpack was on the floor by the bathroom door. I grabbed it and slipped it on as I made my way to the stairs toward the basement level. Greg and

Joseph were catching up with me. I stopped at the end of the stairwell, not knowing which direction to go.

Greg jumped over the stair railing and started heading in the garage's direction, so I followed him, but as I was passing the area Greg jumped, Joseph jumped over the railing and grabbed the backpack which brought me to the ground. I struggled with him. I got on my back because the backpack was nearly empty. The tools pushed on my back. He had me pinned down, so I planted my feet on the ground with my knees bent. I reached with my left arm between his arms and lifted my butt up off the ground, which pushed him forward, moving his arms to the ground above my head. I wrapped my left arm around his arm and took my right hand and placed it on his waist. With all my strength, I pushed him to my left, using my body and my arm to rollover, I was able to get on top of him. Still having my left arm wrapped around his right arm, I squeezed it close to my body, and hit him as hard as I could in his right shoulder with the palm of my hand. His shoulder made a popping sound. Joseph seemed to be in pain. I looked for Greg and found him standing in front of me with his arm out. Joseph was nursing his shoulder giving me the opportunity to escape. I grabbed Greg's hand and pulled myself up. We made it to the garage. I opened my mirror, and we headed back to the Villa.

Twenty-Eight

When we arrived in our room, I drop the backpack to the floor before letting myself fall back on the bed. "Where did he come from?" I tried to catch my breath.

"When I went to the bathroom, he must have heard me. I barely got the door open when he started swinging," Greg said as he sat on the bed next to me. "You were quite impressive back there. I almost jumped in to help you, but you had the situation under control. We must always make sure we are invisible when we are spying on someone. They now know we are up to something."

I knew he was right. I had messed up. We are incredibly lucky we got away. I apologized knowing this was all my fault.

We took a few minutes to collect ourselves before getting the pen out to listen to the recording. As we listened, we heard snoring, followed by what sounded like them getting out of bed. When they started talking, it was about them heading to breakfast and Maria telling him who she had invited over.

The contents of the recording disappointed us. A discussion began about other places to put recordings and cameras. We needed to get more recorders. I will put a recorder in Anthony's car. We went downstairs to talk to Leonardo, but he was busy with the guests and dinner. Greg and I decided the food looked so good we would get something to eat.

We shared an order of Spaghetti alla Carbonara. Leonardo came by to see if we were enjoying our meal. We told him to let Chef Giovanni know it was delicious. Greg explained to Leonardo we needed his help. We headed to our room after dinner and waited for him.

We took turns showering and getting ready for bed. Greg and I made ourselves comfortable. We discussed the events that occurred that day. We also needed to find out if Anthony had an office or if he worked out of the house.

After our discussion, I was drying my hair when I heard Leonardo arrived. I grabbed the robe from the hook in the bathroom and headed to the bedroom to speak with him. We explained our need for a few recording pens and perhaps a few more cameras. Greg showed him the pictures of the items we found in the safe to see if he could translate them. I had forgotten about the pictures and had not seen them yet. Although, I did not remember them being in Italian.

Leonardo looked over the list of items and told us," They seemed to be a list of assets; rare items, probably stolen." As he looked over the contacts, "The people listed have a brief description of skills next to their names." He pointed at one of the names, Piero Rossi, "Fence for stolen goods."

Greg asked him if he could translate the pages in the photo for us. He said he would, and asked us to text them to him, which Greg did. We should have them back tomorrow. He had a lot of paperwork to do and new guests coming the following day he needed to deal with. Leonardo will put the translated document in our room for us. He assured us he would delete the photos. Once he left, we went to bed. As I laid there, my back was bothering me from the tools pressing on it during the struggle. I thought about how I could defend myself. I must admit, I was proud of how much I learned, and I put it into action.

The next morning, we got up and got ready for breakfast. I realized it was Monday and Anthony might head to work, so we headed back to his house to put the pen in his vehicle. We transported to the garage and this time making sure we were invisible. There was a car here that was not there the previous night when we escaped from Joseph. We figured it must have been Anthony's vehicle. I transported myself into the car and put the pen under the passenger's seat. Making sure it was secure and could not roll. I got out, locking the door behind me. We teleported back to our room at the villa and packed up all our things because we had to head home that day. After breakfast, we headed into town for a while to see a bit of Italy, because we could not do any more until we had Leonardo provide us the translated sheets.

We headed to Boboli Gardens, which may have been a mistake. There were a ton of stairs, but it had a spectacular view of Florence. It was a very romantic day walking around enjoying the view and the garden. Greg and I walked hand in hand and occasionally one of us would steal a kiss or two. I wished we could take pictures to remember this day, but we could not have any evidence we were there. We stopped to take in the view when we heard someone say, they're over here. I pivoted around to see the Granaldi brothers heading our way. We were nearly at the top, so we started running back down toward the bottom of the gardens.

It turned out Anthony and Joseph were quickly approaching us. We periodically shifted directions and ran down more stairs, but still making our way to the bottom. I told him to get to the restrooms. When I saw Neptune's fountain, I thought for a second about us using it to teleport, but there was a lot of tourists in the area. It was then I remembered there were a bunch of trees near the amphitheater.

As we were midway down the seating in the amphitheater, I stopped and turned toward a tall wall with hedges in front of it. *Can we make it over?* I knew it would be hard, but I had to try. Greg looked over at me and nodded to tell me he understood what I was thinking. We both made a break for it.

Greg easily made it over, I made it up to the wall and was about to pull myself over when Greg came over to help me. The Granaldi brothers were struggling with the hedges in front of the wall. We turned and headed up the stairs to the top of the stadium. I stopped to check on them. They were still having a hard time getting to the wall. We got to the top and Greg looked around. I looked down. It was a long drop and trees were surrounding us. I told Greg we can make it to the branches.

He agreed and told me to follow him. The trees were very thick, which would make it difficult to get through. I watched Greg jump. He grabbed a branch and made his way to the trunk of the tree. He waited there for me, "Okay, be careful."

I looked and saw the Granaldi brothers made it over the wall and were heading in our direction. My heart was racing. I wiped the sweat off my hands. It terrified me. Greg must have known because he told me to stop thinking and just jump. Without thinking, I went for it. I made it to the branch and could feel the limbs of the tree scratching my body as I jumped. I worked my way to the trunk, making sure I did not lose my grip. When Greg could reach me, he pulled me toward him.

He started to head down the trunk when I told him to stay. I carefully pulled the mirror out of my pocket and flipped it open. Instructing him to hold on and before we knew it; we were back in our room at the villa. I looked at Greg and he had scratches on him too. We went to the bathroom and cleaned ourselves up.

"Greg how are we going to explain this to our parents," I said as I pointed to my scratches.

"We'll say you fell into a thorn bush," Greg suggested.

"How do we both just fall into a thorn bush?" I asked.

He appeared to be thinking for a minute and said, "We were playing flag football and we were on opposite teams and we both went for the ball and did not see the thorn bush," Greg said so convincingly.

"That might just work," I said.

We saw the papers on the dresser that Leonardo left us. It was a list of stolen items, criminal contacts, and Anthony's will. Greg needed a break. We went down and saw Leonardo taking people to their room. It appeared lunch was nearly over, so we asked for them to just give us anything. The server brought out Fettuccine Alfredo and garlic bread. The last few days were a lot to deal with, but it was nearly time to head home. I didn't want to leave. It is no wonder my grandmother loved it here. Greg finished first and said he was going to get the tools and return them to Leonardo. I told him I would meet him in our room. When I finished my lunch, I headed into the building; I heard a commotion at the front desk. I did not want to be nosey, but I could not help but listen.

"I know Brooke Garrison is staying here. Don't make me ask twice," he said forcefully.

"What I am trying to say is, I am not sure she is here at the moment," Isabella picked up the phone. "I have a couple of gentlemen here looking for Ms. Brooke Garrison. Do you know where she is?" There was a pause before she hung up the phone and said, "We believe she went into town for the day."

"Well, we are going to look around anyway," he said.

I hid behind a wall and pulled out my mirror and made myself appear in the same spot, but invisible. I saw the Granaldi brothers heading down the hall. They passed the dining area and were heading toward the wine cellar. I followed them.

The wine cellar door opened, and Leonardo stepped out and greeted them.

"Where is Brooke Garrison?" Tony demanded.

Leonardo stood in front of the cellar door, "She went into town."

Anthony pushed him aside and went into the cellar and looked around. Leonardo started walking toward me.

I whispered, "Leonardo, where is Greg?" He looked around. I told him it was me. "Where is Greg?"

"He is safe. I put him in the safe room," he whispered.

I opened my mirror and went to our room. I grabbed all our things and quickly checked to make sure I had everything before teleporting to the safe room. When I appeared, Greg seemed surprised to see me. We need to get out of here. He grabbed my arm, and we transported to the back of the bus station. We called an Uber and headed back to Nick's house to get my car. On the way back, we discussed things we would tell them we did in Atlanta. I parked the car in my driveway and Greg gave me a kiss goodbye before he headed home. We decided to try to avoid each other for the rest of the day to prevent our parents from asking too many questions about the trip to Atlanta.

To my surprise, Phyllis was not in the kitchen, but she was sitting down and reading a book in the drawing-room. I dropped my backpack on the floor next to me as I plopped down on the chair and started telling her about our trip. After our brief discussion, I headed to my room to change into my bathing suit to get some sun. As I sunned on the third-floor balcony and thought about everything that had happened and everything we still needed to do, I found myself thinking about all that had happened in Italy. How could I ever repay Greg for everything he has taught me? I know I still have a lot to learn. He is such a blessing.

Twenty-Nine

In the following weeks, I got back to the rhythm of school. Greg and I had little contact because Austin needed help on the farm before and after school. Juliet and I have been hanging out a lot after classes. She has even started going to Parkour with me. Juliet works out regularly but said it was the most fun she has ever had working out.

"Greg's Mom lets me come over and use the punching bag despite Greg not being around, which has helped me get stronger every day."

I had not heard from Leonardo and Isabella since we returned; I decided I was going to head back there after class. Juliet and I walked out to our cars, which were normally parked relatively close to one another. We said our goodbyes, and I headed home. I needed to get to Italy and be back before Mom got home. When I arrived at the house, I told Phyllis my plans.

I headed to my room and called Greg to see if he could go with me because we needed to get the pen back from Anthony's car. We also needed to check the recordings. He could not come. Worried about me going alone, he pleaded with me to wait until he was available. He said he would text me when he got home, which he guessed would be around 9:00 pm. I told him it depended on my mother.

I went to see Leonardo and Isabella about the items we requested while I waited for Greg. To not stand out during the dinner hour, I changed into an appropriate outfit before heading to my room in the villa. One last look in the full-length mirror before looking for them. I heard laughter coming from the dining room as I made my way down the stairs. I peeked in but did not see Leonardo, so I headed toward the front to see if I could find Isabella. She was mopping up the floor at the front entrance. "Brooke!" she said as she realized I was back at the villa. She put the mop down and gave me a hug. "We have been so worried about you and Greg."

I assured her we were fine. She told me the Granaldis had been back several times looking for us, but they had not been around in a week. She pulled me closer to her room, out of earshot of anyone. "Leonardo procured something you really needed that is of great value," Isabella informed me.

It took me a minute, but she must be referring to the drug I needed. "That's wonderful. Where's Leonardo?" I asked.

She told me he was either in the dining room or the kitchen. I headed back to the dining room, which we had never eaten in, but it was a beautiful room. They packed the room with people because of the foul weather. I did not see him in the dining room, so I went into the kitchen.

I walked in and found Chef Giovanni busy making meals and it appeared his Sous Chef had cut himself and Leonardo was cleaning out his wound. Everyone was so busy that no one noticed me entering the kitchen. I walked over to Leonardo and said, "Hello."

He leaned toward me and gave me a kiss on the cheek and asked me to get a pair of rubber gloves for him. I got the gloves so he could finish bandaging the Sous Chef's hand. Once finished, he handed the Sous Chef the gloves. He asked me to follow him.

We went to his room, and he motioned for me to have a seat in the sitting area before he went to a closet to get a box. He placed the box on the table in front of me and said, "Everything you asked for is in here." He reached into the box and pulled out a tiny bottle, and said, "This is the Rohypnol you requested. There is only one dose in this bottle. He needs to drink all of this if possible. Make sure you are wearing gloves and have your hair and things up when you are at their home. They now know you have been there. I do not think they will call the police on you, but it is better not to leave any evidence. Even though they cannot see you, we do not know if you leave fingerprints when you touch things. Oh, I nearly forgot. Don't bring your phone when you teleport because it tracks your location and if a picture is taken it can be traced back to the location."

We had been taking our phones with us frequently. This was good advice. "Thank you for the advice and for all of these things." I glanced in the box and saw more recording pens and cameras.

"Isabella said the Granaldis have been back here several times. You need to be careful with them." Leonardo said as he rubbed his ear.

Leonardo informed me he had been dealing with them for years. He assured me he was not in any danger with them. I told him I needed to head back before my mother got home. I grabbed the box and headed back to Kentucky.

When I got back, I asked Phyllis if I could put the box in her room because I did not want to take a chance of my mother discovering it among my things. I knew she would not go through Phyllis's room. I put the box on the floor in the corner of her closet.

My mother got home at 7:35 pm. She informed us at dinner that she is going on a date on Saturday with a man she met at a restaurant she eats lunch at. She explained they have run into each other several times. I was glad to see my mother so excited. She had not been on a date in a long time. She also told us she was heading to her room after dinner to work and would turn in for the night once she finished.

I texted Greg to let him know I was available when he got home. I went to my room to work on my homework until Greg arrived. It was nearly 9:30 pm when he showed up. Phyllis had sent him up to my room. We agreed we were only going to get the pen and replace it with another pen. We also decided to return the painting to the museum it was stolen from. I grabbed another pen from Phyllis's closet, and we tested it to make sure it worked. Greg had all the supplies we would need including our disguises for the museum in his backpack before we left.

We appeared in a corner of the garage away from the vehicles. Tony, with the painting in his hands, walked toward the trunk of Anthony's vehicle, and placed it inside the trunk. I moved over to get a better view of where the painting was inside the trunk. Joseph was about to shut the trunk and Tony stopped him. Anthony entered the garage and asked Tony where the painting was. He pointed to it. Anthony checked it as well. He seemed to approve of how Tony placed it in the trunk. They got in the vehicle and pulled out of the garage.

Per our plan, I teleported to the trunk. I made sure I arrived on the side of the trunk that did not have the painting because I did not want to damage it. I grabbed the painting and returned to Greg.

To make it more difficult for the police to determine our size, we put on black masks and black ponchos. I was also wearing sneakers with heels. I did not find them attractive, but they made me appear taller. My pants covered them to give the illusion I was taller than I was. We put on rubber gloves and wiped the painting of fingerprints. Using an image found online, we popped into the museum, making sure we were visible so the painting would be as well. We wanted the surveillance cameras to see us return the painting. My step triggered the alarm. I placed the painting on a bench in the room. My heart raced from fear they would catch us. We huddled together to hide the mirror from the cameras before transporting to the vineyard.

We arrived at the vineyard before the Granaldi family. I could not wait to see their reaction to seeing the painting missing. We waited hidden in the vineyard off the roadway and spent our time trying to figure out when we could get the Bloom's Cradle and catching up on everything that had been going on while he was working at the farm. We were talking about Mom's date when a car pulled down the dirt road. It stopped not too far from us, but not close enough for us to hear them clearly, so we quietly moved closer to hear the conversation.

A few minutes later another car pulled in. As it got closer to us, we realized the second vehicle was Anthony's. Once Anthony and his sons got out of the car, the passengers of the other vehicle got out. The man from the other vehicle was carrying a duffle bag. Anthony asked him if he had the funds. The man put the duffle bag on the trunk of Anthony's car and opened it.

Anthony seemed satisfied and motioned to Tony to open the trunk. The man took the bag off the trunk. Tony popped the trunk open. When the trunk opened, Anthony was looking at the man, not in the trunk.

The man said, "Is this a joke?" His partner pulled out a gun and aimed it at Anthony's forehead.

Anthony and his boys looked so confused. Anthony turned and looked in the trunk. His face seemed shocked, "It's not here!" He looked through the trunk. He began apologizing to the man.

The man informed him he would not be doing business with him in the future and was going to get the word out about the type of business he does and headed to his car. Anthony and the boys said nothing and got back in their car and drove off. I told Greg we needed to get back to their house to get the Bloom's Cradle.

When we got to the house, we waited in the basement to see where they would go. When they finally arrived, they headed to the bar in the basement. Anthony poured himself a drink as he ranted about me. He kept saying. "I know Brooke took it. How else would it just disappear from the trunk?" He put his drink down and headed to the bathroom. I tiptoed over to his drink and slipped the Rohypnol into it.

He returned from the bathroom and grabbed his drink and started heading toward the elevator. We quickly but quietly made our way up the spiral staircase to the first floor. He went into the living room and joined his wife, who was watching television.

   Anthony filled her in on what had occurred at the meeting as he continued to drink his cocktail. The more he drank, he started getting exhausted. He told his wife he was going to bed. She told him she would be there as soon as her show was over.

He walked through the ball room to his bedroom and shut the door, so we teleported into the sitting room area of the master suite. He sat down on his bed and looked at his shoes before he leaned back and was sound asleep. Greg and I tried to get the ring off his finger, but it did not budge. I went to the bathroom and found liquid soap. Greg held his finger while I squirted soap on it. I rolled the ring around in the soap to make it easier to remove the ring. Anthony stirred for a moment. My heart jumped. I continued moving the ring until it came off his finger. *We got it!* I put the soap back and wiped the soap off his finger with tissues I found in the bathroom. I brought the tissues with us to ensure we left no evidence behind.

Thirty

When we arrived back in my room, we started looking at the ring. The ring had a type of cage on it. The stone must sit inside, but I could not figure out how to open it. Greg took the ring and started inspecting it. He looked like he was trying to pull the top of the ring off.

"Be careful," I warned.

He popped the top of the ring off. It looked like a small cage that would hold the Bloom of Dreams.

Greg asked me for my necklace and started inspecting it, "Did you notice this?" He pointed to what looked like a unique lock in the silver that surrounded the stone.

I told him I had never noticed it and asked him to unlock it. He was able to open it and took the stone from the necklace and placed it in the Bloom's Cradle. Greg and I looked at each other as if to say, "That's it." I think we both thought it would be a more dramatic moment. Greg helped me attach the Bloom's Cradle that now held the Bloom of Dreams to the chain and placed it on my neck. I noticed no change. He took it back and put it on the ring. I put the ring on, but it was large enough to fit a big man. We noticed when he put the stone on the necklace it could touch my skin through the bottom of the Cradle. We put the cradle back on my chain because the ring was way too large. I walked over to the full-length mirror and pictured myself in my bathroom, and my bathroom appeared in the mirror. I stepped through it and was in the bathroom.

"It still works," I walked back into my bedroom. "I guess we are going to need to wait and see if it does anything else." I was disappointed by how uneventful this moment was.

The next day on the news we saw a report about the Le Pigeon Aux Petits Pois being returned to the museum they stole it from. The reporter explained, "Our source said two people magically appeared in the museum. They put the painting on a bench, and they vanished from the museum. The police believe they are some sort of magicians." *They are searching for two magicians.* I felt proud of our accomplishment.

Greg and I made dinner for Phyllis because Mom was out with Lance. Greg was chopping up vegetables to put in the salad when he sliced his finger open. He put his finger under the water and as I was inspecting it; I noticed he cut it deep.

"I think you're going to need stitches," I said as I watched the blood flowing. He was in a lot of pain. I dried the water off his hand, but the stone warmed as I was applying pressure to his finger. I looked around to see if the Granaldi's were outside, but I did not see anyone.

Greg said, "It stopped hurting."

"What do you mean it stopped hurting?" I asked.

"When you put your hand on the cut, it warmed up and then felt better," he said.

I removed my hand, and the paper towel from his finger and the cut was gone. *How could that be?*

Greg and I realized the stone with the cradle could heal a person. We did not know if it did anything else, but we were excited about our new discovery.

Over the next few weeks, we took Phyllis and her Derby Pie to Italy to see Leonardo and Isabella. We had a wonderful evening with them. They informed us none of the Granaldi family had been to the villa, but they knew them, and they were planning something. Greg and I continued working on my skills. Mom was officially dating Lance, but I still had not met him because she wanted to see where the relationship was going before introducing us. Mom liked the stone in my new necklace, but I think she missed seeing the necklace her mother always wore.

Greg and I were doing well and hoped there were more secrets to discover about the Bloom of Dreams and how the cradle affected it. We had returned several times to listen to the recordings and discovered the Granaldis were fuming about the painting and the ring being taken. We were sure they would be back soon, but until then we are not letting our guard down.

By D.A. Dwinell
The Bloom's Cradle - Guardian of the Stone - Book 2
Bloom Keepers - Guardian of the Stone - Book 3

Connect with D.A. Dwinell
If you want the latest news on D.A. Dwinell or interested in connecting on social media, please visit the following site:
www.facebook.com/DADwinell

Made in the USA
Columbia, SC
01 April 2022